'This moving, unique, incredibly assured debut is
full of life's slow richness, the lagging toll of grief
and the brightness of unconditional love.'
Guardian

'A phenomenal book. Such a distinctive voice,
so beautifully crafted, and what a premise.'
Louisa Reid

'Fresh, hopeful and thought-provoking
and with a real lightness of touch.'
Rashmi Sirdeshpande

'A poignant debut with a punch-packing, end-of-the-
world set-up, and unconditional love at its heart. Through
its deeply endearing characters, this tells a stirring story
of family finding a way through loss, loneliness and
feeling abandoned to embrace what's really important.'
Lovereading.co.uk

'A breathtaking debut about hope, healing and love.'
The Bookseller

'I picked it up and couldn't stop. It's beautiful – original,
emotionally truthful and infused with love and hope.'
Patrice Lawrence

'It's good to meet kindness in books – a rare commodity
– and humanity at its best. A beautiful debut about
finding the light even as the world is ending'
Jenny Downham

THE CATS WE MEET ALONG THE WAY
is a GUPPY BOOK

First published in the UK in 2022 by
Guppy Books,
Bracken Hill,
Cotswold Road,
Oxford OX2 9JG

Text copyright © Nadia Mikail
Inside illustrations © Nate Ng

978 1 913101 596

5 7 9 10 8 6

Papers used by Guppy Books are from well-managed
forests and other responsible sources.

MIX
Paper | Supporting
responsible forestry
FSC® C171272

GUPPY PUBLISHING LTD Reg. No. 11565833

A CIP catalogue record for this book is
available from the British Library.

Typeset by Falcon Oast Graphic Art Ltd
Printed and bound in Great Britain by CPI Books Ltd

THE CATS WE MEET ALONG THE WAY

NADIA MIKAIL

Illustrations by Nate Ng

GUPPY BOOKS

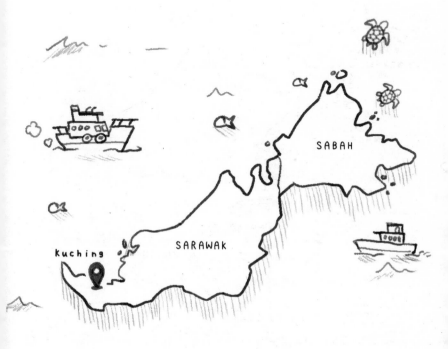

Aisha's family
used to live
in kuching.

For Child

The Cat, Part One

(the present)

The cat that followed them home had a bald patch on his left hind leg and one ear missing. It was orange, a distasteful, dirty shade of it, one that reminded Aisha of fish curry gone off.

"Shoo," Aisha told it. The cat ignored her.

"Don't be mean," Walter said, reproachfully. He leaned down and flashed his crooked canines at it, bent his dark head to look properly. "Kitty, are you lost?"

"Mew," said the cat impatiently, which to Aisha sounded like it meant *obviously not, I'm following you to my new home.*

When Walter got up and they rounded the corner to her street, the cat followed steadily, like it was inherently familiar with the place.

"Oh, it probably has fleas," she protested, making a more vigorous shooing motion.

"I don't think it matters," said Walter. He meant, *since we're all going to die anyway*. "I don't want it to be alone when . . . well. When."

Still, Aisha would rather die with her scalp not itching, thank you very much. She opened their lime green front door and said, "Hi, Mak."

"Hi, *sayang*," said her mother, looking up from the lined exercise book she used for recipes. The sun struggled through the grimy windowpane, on its last legs. Everything was on its last legs these days, it seemed. "Hi, Walter. Hi, stray cat I don't want in my kitchen."

Aisha looked at Walter and shrugged not-very-regretfully. "You heard her. Her kitchen, her rules."

But Walter looked at her mother, and Aisha knew it

was a lost cause already. They exchanged a glance in which Walter communicated to Esah plaintive sentences about not wanting the cat to be alone at the End, his gaze beseeching, and Aisha could see the moment when her mother's eyes softened. A beat later Esah asked, "So what's his name?"

"It's a he?"

Esah gestured towards where the cat was sitting on the doormat, licking clear evidence of he-dom.

"Hm," said Walter. "What's his name, Sha?"

"Fleabag," said Aisha.

Walter flicked her ear gently, thumb and index finger. "Don't be so mean."

"You know, I think it'll stick," Aisha's mother said. She smiled absently in the direction of Fleabag, who made a huge show of a ragged lick to his nether regions, as if to illustrate the point.

"Fleabag," Walter said, crouching over him and scritching at his chin. "Don't worry about her. Think of it as a fond nickname."

Aisha was watching her mother, who was still looking vaguely at the cat. She wondered what Esah was thinking about. June had told her, once, that strays had used to follow her father home as well, close at his heels, rubbing their heads against his ankles. Perhaps Esah was remembering them in Fleabag's furry face.

The Cat, Part Two

(the present)

Perhaps the problem was that they might have gotten married if the world was not ending. Aisha could see it sometimes, arrayed in front of her, the progression of their decades: the engagement, the house, the dog, the first kid's wide grin, the second's chubby fists. Lazy mornings, her favourite bowl of *laksa* brought to her in bed, packing their lunches for work, Sunday evenings at the neighbour-hood park.

She would have been happy too. They would have been delirious with it, that uncomplicated happiness. Now they were fighting more than ever, eight months before the world ended. Aisha would have named her first child Amin after her beloved uncle, her father's favourite brother. Walter would have loved that name because of all the stories she'd told him of Uncle Amin and how he'd taken her to the swings every Friday before he'd died. Aisha would have gone to school and tried to help people who were in pain. Walter would have meandered from career to career, indecisive and passionate about everything. Aisha would have wanted to travel the world. They would have had a number of cats because Walter wouldn't have been able to say no to strays who followed them home.

Walter cooed silly things at Fleabag, now sitting at her mother's kitchen table, and Aisha loved him, loved him desperately, loved him more than anything.

"You know," Esah said, her low voice cutting smoothly into Aisha's thoughts, "I've been thinking about June." She said it very carefully, like it was just another thing on the grocery list she wanted Aisha to get. Both Aisha and Walter's heads snapped up. Fleabag, who clearly couldn't

6

stand the attention not being on him for a second, jumped gracefully onto the floor and padded away.

Like it was his own house. Aisha supposed abstractly that now it was.

"Oh?" Aisha said, just as careful. She felt rooted to the spot, felt something clawing at her throat, wasn't sure if it was panic. "Everything okay? Did you hear some news?"

"No, I didn't hear anything." Esah put her blue mixing bowl down, into the sink, and ran the tap. She wasn't looking at it. The bowl still contained all the batter she needed for the cake. "I was just thinking that I want to make things right," she said. "What with, you know, everything."

"Everything," Aisha repeated uselessly. "So you want to go to her?" Walter's head turned back and forth, as if he was watching a tennis match.

"Maybe," said Esah. The water flowed down into the batter, ugly, and Esah looked at it, unseeing. "What else can I do?" She meant, *now that we have no time left.*

7

Aisha walked over to her mother's side and put her arms around her very, very gently. She reached forward and turned off the tap. The batter lay there, embarrassed and ruined. Esah let out a loud annoyed sniff and muttered about the loss of cake.

"What else can *we* do, you mean, Mak," Aisha said. "I'm with you." She ignored whatever it was that was clawing inside her and nodded firmly, forehead against her mother's warm shoulder, trying to be convincing. "One step at a time. It'll all be okay."

A Story about June

(three years ago)

June had been nineteen when she'd decided she'd had enough of the house.

"What do you mean you've had enough of the house?" Aisha had demanded, following her around the room as she picked up things, considered them carefully, and either threw them back down or into her suitcase.

Her suitcase was fading and huge and still shockingly pink. June had pleaded for it when she was sixteen, for her trip to Europe. Their mother had given in to the trip after a month of June alternating between furiously sulking and sweetly doing every chore in the house. She had made

June install a tracking app on her phone, so she could check that she was at exactly the places she'd said she'd be, at exactly the times she'd said she'd be at them.

"I just . . ." June considered her sister, her suitcase, her stuffed dinosaur, Lala. "It's not the house. The house is a metaphor."

"We're not in English class, June!" Aisha had been fifteen and distressed. She watched as June picked up a pair of socks and discarded them firmly into the depths of her wardrobe. "What does that mean? A metaphor for what?"

June stopped short and stared at her, as if it was obvious. "For how if I don't leave now I'll stay my whole life," she said.

"You won't, you're supposed to go to university!"

"University schmuniversity," June declared, succinctly. She'd finished her last A level that day. As Aisha recalled, it had been Literature, hence the metaphor talk. "I'm not going. I just haven't told Mak and you since you'd both be on my case and this way I got to enjoy these last few months with you both . . . I'm not dying, Sha. I'll still be your sister."

At this she sat down on her (faded pink) bed and held firmly onto Aisha's shoulders like she would never let go (she had). "I'm just . . . finding myself."

Aisha stared at June, the almost manic glint in her eyes, the (bright pink) highlights in her hair. "You can do that here."

"I know I can't," June said, stubbornly sure about this like she was stubbornly sure about most things.

"What will Mak say?" Aisha asked, a last-ditch attempt. She was fifteen and too fifteen to say *please don't leave me. Not yet.*

"Ah," said June, looking away. "There's the rub. If she could only understand – but she'd never – but you never know, she might." She rubbed at her chin, unsure. Then she looked back at Aisha with something like hope. "Maybe if you said something. Maybe that would help?"

"You want me to say something," Aisha said slowly, "to make her okay with you leaving?"

"She listens to you," June said, which was blatantly untrue in Aisha's opinion. "You're the good child. Say something so she isn't so upset?"

"There's nothing I can say that'll do that," Aisha said flatly. But June, shrugging away Aisha's doubt, seemed to take this as confirmation of her help. She spun around a little happier, tossing a hairbrush into her luggage.

She'd told their mother that night, over dinner. Esah had asked, *What about university*? Esah had said, *You're too young to know what you want*. Esah had shouted, and she rarely shouted, *Leave now and you leave for ever. Go, then!* Sik kenang budi.

A silence had fallen that had somehow been worse than the many and prolonged silences they'd had in that little house. June had said nothing. Aisha had felt her eyes on her, her stare burning a hole through her head. The gaze had felt like something pleading, something hot and pained. Aisha had stared at the fried fish and willed herself far away from here. She willed it so hard she imagined she couldn't feel the stare any more. They'd sat silently at the table until the plates were empty, then June had washed the dishes and gone upstairs.

An hour later they'd watched the shockingly pink suitcase trundle down their footpath, June's bright pink highlighted head bent low but steady, leading it away.

There was a wound in Aisha that had opened up steadily with every visible step her sister took away from her. She had lost people, but those people hadn't wanted to go. June had chosen to leave. She had chosen to disappear from their lives without a trace, and she had chosen not to come back.

Walter, Leaving

(the present)

"I think I'd better go," said Walter. "Ma's expecting me."

"Bye, Walter," Esah said distractedly, flapping her fingers at him. "Be safe."

Esah loved Walter, in the way that almost everyone who met Walter loved Walter: whole-heartedly and slightly surprised about it, like they hadn't realised they'd started when they had, but now they wouldn't want it any other way.

"Bye, Auntie," Walter said politely. He waved back and scritched Fleabag's chin, used the other sink to run the tap and wash his hands, and let Aisha walk him out the door.

*

Aisha knew exactly when and how she'd begun to love Walter. There was no suddenness about it, no tide coming in she hadn't realised. One night Walter had texted her, *hey can I call you about this*? instead of texting, and they'd talked till dawn. Talked about *Antony and Cleopatra* and *As You Like It*, which they were studying in class, but also about his parents, her mak, his dog, her lack of pets, his fondness for trashy reality television, her favourite Tolkien novel. She told him about the time she'd fallen heavily from the monkey bars in kindergarten and gone crying to her big sister. He told her about the time his mother had forgotten about him in the Sunday market and he'd sat there amongst the produce until she came back and gathered him up in her arms. Her secret fear of blood she was studiously trying to get past. His fumbling first date at Kafe Baluddin. She told him she wanted to go out into the world and see every place she could, and she always felt incredibly guilty about that desire. He told her he

15

wanted to be a writer and a mathematician and a marine biologist, that the world seemed so full of things he could do but that there always seemed so little time to do them.

She'd put down the phone and said to herself, "Well, then."

And it wasn't even that she thought he was perfect. It had been two years. She knew that he ate with his mouth open and he was indecisive beyond words. She knew he was determined to wear his holey sneakers until they fell apart in the street one day and he sometimes took his parents for granted. She knew he could be spoiled and snappish and as stubborn as she was, and she loved all of this fiercely and on purpose. From that first call it had always been his voice, warm like her most-loved armchair, warm like new laundry, warm like the Sunday morning kitchen with her mother baking, humming, alive.

"Tomorrow?" asked Aisha.

"Tomorrow," Walter said, bending down to nuzzle

softly at her cheek, the sensation light and slightly ticklish. Lifting his head after a moment, he poked affectionately at her neck, her jaw, her stomach, faster and faster until she was giggling and swatting at him.

"You're a child," she informed him. "This is what children do."

"It's going to be okay," Walter said in reply, putting his arms around her. He did not treat her like she was fragile, because they weren't. He squeezed until the worry, for a moment, leeched away in a trickle: slowly, but so very thoroughly. It was Walter's way: certain he could do impossible things like leak all her problems away if he set his mind to it. He wasn't wrong. Walter, Aisha was certain, would have been no match for the world, given time. He would have written and counted and deep-sea dived, and then he would have been hungry for more.

When he pulled away, Aisha could still feel the lingering sensation on her skin: the nudge of his nose, the brief brush of his lips.

"I love you," Walter said, careless with it. He flashed a sweet easy smile at her. "After lunch. Three."

"All right," Aisha said. "Okay."

An Explanation

(four months ago)

The world found out it was ending on just another Tuesday.

IN A YEAR, the headlines screamed. Back when there had still been headlines. An asteroid heading straight for collision, Hollywood-perfect for the end of the world. It really was like something out of a movie. Sometimes it still felt like a cruel, extended prank.

When the news was announced, Aisha had been out with Walter on the beach, everything swathed in golden light, the waves coming in, going out, coming in again. They'd driven out for the weekend, phones left at home. They'd been laughing when people had started screaming. Then the beach had emptied like the tide rolling back, quick.

Aisha had thought: *tsunami*. She'd thought: *bombing, financial collapse, mass shooting*. Then they'd gotten into the car and driven home silently, and Esah had met them at the lime green front door and her face had been pale, her hands shaking. Aisha had realised it was all those things at once, and the end of all those things at once.

Here was how the end of the world was predicted to play out:

The world wreathed in fire and smoke, everything burning.

Earthquakes and tsunamis shuddering, cracking, shifting what was left.

Volcanoes erupting, water corrosive, the very air poison, and what was left dark, the sun sheathed in unlight.

It turned out that governments had known about it for four years, and planned everything from deflecting the path of the asteroid, to frantically focusing their efforts on space, to attempting to build large underground bunkers – but when none of it seemed like it was going to work, they had all addressed their people at the same time.

These times are dark, the speeches all started, *but one thing is to be remembered: the power of humanity to come together and face what is to come is undefeated.* Most of the world had watched the broadcast, a video that had popped up while they were scrolling through their timeline or across their screen during their nightly binge-watch. Some people had heard it on the radio, and some on their smartwatches. Some people had woken up to the news.

Most people immediately started digging bunkers or building shelters. Scientists came on the news to say that even the strongest ones wouldn't be much use against an asteroid miles-wide, trust them, they'd checked. They teleconferenced in from all over the world: *Spend time with your loved ones. Make the most of what's left. Say your prayers.* Their faces had been set and resigned, their opinions reasoned and fact-checked: they were the few who had spent years desperately scrabbling, after all.

That was when there was still news to watch. Slowly it had all stopped, as people gave up on hope. What passed for news these days was the radio, still scrambling messages and music from people trying to reach out to the world and entertain it.

There had been a time, right after the news broke, when there had been plenty of violence and fury and desperation. There had been a period of rioting for food and essentials. Systems of government and law enforcement collapsed. Aisha and Esah spent a month or so primarily inside with the doors and windows locked and barricaded, the very air unspoken with worry and June's name. The stories they heard were brutal ones. There were people setting things on fire, frustrated and despairing with how much of their lives they had worked and how little there was left to show for it. There were other people who resorted to brutality for no reason but because they could.

And then there were the stories of the people who had just given up on their lives.

Time went on, and things shifted. There was still cause to be careful now. People were still angry and anguished. But the larger part of the world ventured out. They started stocking up, growing food and working together to trade items. Communities were created, pockets of people who worked together to survive in the time they had left.

It settled because people realised what was important: good health, no hunger and going home to family. People still worked at these jobs on a voluntary basis, doing their part to help. People made sure enough lines were up for people to call their families far away. People made sure there was enough medicine, food and ways for loved ones to visit each other. If there was the occasional violence and hurt, the community worked together as best it could to protect and defend each other from it.

They all knew the world would end soon. This fact might have driven them all to despair, and in fact it *had* driven some to utter hopelessness, their will to keep going sputtering out like a candle in a ruthless gust of wind.

But many kept on doing what they could, while they were still around, while life lasted. They knew what was important.

They knew that they were doing this for each other.

The Decision

(the present)

Aisha watched Walter walk away. She watched him turn the corner at the end of the road and she watched the sky turn to pale pink and deeper blues. Then she walked back, opened their bright green door and said, "Mak?"

"In here," Esah said.

Aisha walked to her mother's room, pushing Fleabag away with her foot when he tried to follow. "You don't belong here," she whispered to him.

Fleabag scowled, in as much as a cat could.

Esah was sitting on her bed. She looked almost startled

when Aisha appeared in the doorway. "*Sayang*," she said. "Hungry?"

"Mak," said Aisha.

Esah spread her palms open on her lap and just looked at them. "I don't even know where she is."

June had not made any attempt to contact them after that last day. Esah had not looked for her, as far as Aisha knew. Aisha had not, because it was June who had left. June was the one who could have come back any time.

They hadn't talked about her at all after she'd left. Esah had taken down the picture frames with her in them – Aisha came home one day and found them all gone – and Esah never put them back up. The spaces that were left on the drawers and walls felt like holes, but Aisha and Esah wiped away the dust that accumulated on the surfaces where they had been. There had to be clean new skin; left-open wounds became infected.

Losing June had hurt like a wound at first, and then Aisha tried very hard not to think about it. The scar had raised itself in time and Aisha didn't pick at it, because it was new skin and you didn't pick at new skin.

"We can try to find her," Aisha said, and even here, three years later, the scar felt like it would split open. "We could. I think I know where she is. Where she could be."

They stood there in the bedroom. If Aisha squinted she could easily recall the many memories of her mother curled up on this bed, under this blanket, staring into space. Aisha didn't spend much time in this room, even these days when these occurrences were rare.

"We can try," Esah agreed, looking up from her hands. They didn't say *We have to try, there is no other choice.* There was only so much new skin could take.

After Lunch

(the present)

When Aisha climbed into bed that night she couldn't sleep for a long time, so she stopped trying: she just lay down with her eyes open and stared out the window at the moon. She thought, as she often did, of the moment before the tide went out and the people emptied the shore, when Walter had said, "Pass me a Magnum – no, a Walls. Actually, a Magnum, please," and she had reached over and laughed when she'd come up with what felt like mush in the packet. Their ice creams had melted. Their cooler had not been closed properly.

They'd been able to laugh about it. If something like that happened now, Aisha would snap that *one* of them should have been more careful and Walter would go closed-off, also snippy, but curt and short with it.

But back then they'd been able to laugh at it. Walter had giggled and torn open the wrapper and tilted the ruined ice cream into his mouth to make her laugh more, getting melted ice everywhere. Aisha had said, "Ew, no don't do that, ew!" and Walter had reached the mush dangerously over to her face . . .

Aisha fell asleep, between this moment and the next.

She overslept, which was strange. Before the Announcement, the way everyone said it with the capital A quiet in their mouths, Aisha had been all of a seventeen-year-old student, who treasured deeply her lie-ins and whose mother shouted about breakfast to wake her up. Now time was precious. She woke up early and faced the day and whatever would come with it.

Still today she overslept, and awoke to Esah shaking her shoulder gently.

"Bangun, sayang."

The sunlight had made its relentless way through her window, and Aisha winced when she opened her eyes. The sun seemed brighter these days: brighter and so very tired, all at once. Like a final spurt of a sprint. Like it knew it was the final stretch.

"What time is it?"

"One," Esah said. "Lunchtime." She went downstairs.

Lunch was carrots from the garden and one of Mrs Liew's chickens, freshly slaughtered and plucked and turned into *kurma*. They ate quietly, but there was still . . . something. Something had changed, from yesterday. Like the air was humming.

Aisha had thought they would spend their last days in this little house. Or, to be entirely truthful: she hadn't really thought about it, or talked about it with Esah, what with getting used to this strange pre-apocalyptic world. They still might spend their last days in this little house, but *June,* the name like a scab, like a scar, now hung in the air. She could be anywhere, and they were going to find her.

Perhaps the air was humming with small adventure.

Aisha was washing the dishes when Walter knocked on the door. Three polite knocks, as always, then he waited for someone to answer.

Esah said, "I'll take care of the rest, go answer the door," and Aisha gratefully stepped back, wringing her hands, and went outside.

Walter smiled at her. He was wearing a shirt with a dog on it, faded blue and one of his favourites. He was wearing his sneakers that were falling apart, the ones Aisha hated.

Aisha loved him immensely. That was why it spilled out of her, why she said, "We're going to find June." Her stomach was turning with it. "Walter," she said, "please come with us."

Walter was a person of much deliberation. He loved many things in the world, like ice cream and cartoon animal T-shirts and coral documentaries and his trumpet. He jumped from interest to interest, devouring them all and firmly not deciding on something silly like A Single Career. This also meant it took ages for him to decide things like what to eat for dinner, because he wanted to try everything he saw on the menu, or which playlist to listen to in the car, which meant in the end they didn't listen to more than thirty seconds of one song.

Walter said, with no hesitation, "Okay."

Her eyes must have been wide because he said again, laughing, "Okay," and "Yes," and "Of course," and gathered her close into his arms. He smelled of his familiarly woodsy cologne, something so safe and dependable. She closed her eyes in relief.

"Aisha, I need my parents to come along," he said, mouth moving against her hair.

"Of course," Aisha said into his warm, solid chest, feeling more than a little overwhelmed and more than a lot grateful.

When he smiled, she could feel it. "Will you come with me to ask them?"

"Okay," Aisha said, feeling like she'd agree to anything he asked right then. "Yes. Of course."

Walter's Parents, Part One

(two years and a month ago)

The first time Aisha had met Robert Gan and Elizabeth Jelani, she'd been slightly wary.

Dating someone of a different race was not the easiest thing, at least not in Malaysia. It was a thing families still tended to think twice about because of the long, tense racial history wrapped into their nationhood, a place where religion figured heavily when two people of different races thought about marriage. It was worry wrapped up in fear, and Aisha knew that this was a volatile package.

So the first time Aisha had met Robert Gan and Elizabeth Jelani, she'd been cautious.

Walter had reassured her over and over again. *They're great, you know, for parents,* had been one of his most frequent refrains, along with *You're wonderful and they'll love you,* another favourite. He'd reminded her of this at the cinema, in the car, on the phone, hopeful and earnest about it.

Eventually Aisha had not managed to put it off any longer. Walter had said, "Yeah, maybe next time," very quietly, the last time Aisha suggested maybe another date for the first meeting, and his eyes had been cast down, lashes dark against his cheeks. Aisha hated herself a little bit for that. It was important to be brave if it meant she didn't have to see that look ever again.

"Actually," she'd said. "Actually. Tomorrow's fine."

Walter's smile, with its crooked canines, slowly spread.

The next afternoon, Aisha had stepped cautiously into the compound of Walter's semi. Her little house had a small patch of grass in front and a couple of pots in the back, but

Walter had a garden: one with a mango tree and wild, soft grass. One time, madly passionate about rodent behaviour for a month, he'd set up a maze for squirrels. The vestiges of this particular endeavour still lived on in a squirrel feeder by the porch. A white swing rocked lazily in the slight breeze.

Elizabeth Jelani stepped out in a lavender sundress, shielding her eyes from the afternoon, and said to Walter, "Finally! Go spray down the car, it's too hot to think." To Aisha, she said, "Hello!"

"Hi, Auntie," Aisha said, very politely.

Elizabeth Jelani smiled. She was small and slender with straight black hair, tied back, and slightly crooked teeth just like Walter's. She said, "Ah, it's so hot. Let him stay here and spray." She considered Aisha for a fleeting moment, but Aisha felt it: that quick flickering of her quick, kind gaze. "We'll go inside and drink juice."

Walter said "Ugh," perfunctorily, pressed his arm against hers, for a moment, and went. His mother and Aisha went inside and drank juice.

Aisha had never been inside Walter's house before, but she supposed she shouldn't have been surprised that it was covered with pictures of Walter, their only child, beloved son. Everything was very tasteful, with cool colours highlighted by red Chinese New Year decorations that hadn't yet been taken down. There was a piano in the living room, an *engkerumung* near it, and fruits on every surface. They had sat in the kitchen, drinking orange juice – freshly squeezed only that morning! – and Elizabeth asked very casual questions about school and her mother and her sister.

Aisha had stumbled over that last bit. June's departure had still been eleven months fresh at the time, and the anniversary of it was coming up. The question caught her by surprise. "She, uh . . . she moved away."

Elizabeth said, "Oh, they grow up so fast," very quickly and easily, and moved on to a different topic. Then Robert Gan had appeared in the doorway. He was solidly built, like Walter; had Walter's soft thick hair and strong eyebrows.

"Orange juice today!" he said. "Very healthy." He grinned at Aisha, before getting a cup for himself. "Did you know we have three juice makers?"

"They're blenders," Elizabeth said, sounding long-suffering, but smiling.

"Of course. That's what I said. Aisha, is it?"

"Hi, Uncle," Aisha said, very politely.

"I hope Walter is watering the grass too," Robert had said comfortably, coming to sit down beside his wife. "It's such a hot day. Everything's drying out. So," and this was directed to Aisha, "what are you planning to study in uni?"

Aisha said, "Probably medicine. I think. If I get the grades. I don't know yet if I will."

"That's fine," said Robert. "At least you have some idea. I didn't know what I was going to study in uni even after I'd finished studying it. Walter certainly doesn't."

Elizabeth had looked at him fondly. "*Anang majak ka perangai nya.* He already thinks being meandering is fine."

"Being meandering *is* fine," Robert had said. "All roads lead somewhere." He had shaken his head at Aisha. "Even when they're long and winding."

Aisha had sat amidst all this kindness, feeling a little out of place, a little unfamiliar. She then understood, a little better, how Walter had turned out the way he had.

Walter's Parents, Part Two
(the present)

Now Aisha stood outside Walter's semi, thinking that she was asking too much from these people who had made her feel so welcome for two years, despite all their worry. There were only a few months of their lives left, and she was asking them to join a hunt for her sister. Her sister who had left, voluntarily, who had taken steady steps away from her and not looked back.

She thought of the look on her mother's face. And of Walter, of how it was important to be brave for him. For these two people, she would try.

Walter called, unlocking the gate, "Ma. Dad!"

"What a nice surprise," Elizabeth said, opening their front door. "Walter, don't shout, the neighbours."

Elizabeth's reaction to the world ending had been to transform their compound, already teeming with large oranges and lush mangoes and long bananas, into a proper food garden, with bright tomatoes and smooth eggplant and spilling spinach. Chickens clucked furiously, contained in some netting in the back. She gave most of the food away to the neighbourhood and didn't ask for much in return.

Robert's reaction to the world ending had been to quit his engineering job immediately and help his wife with the garden.

They sat down at the kitchen table. Elizabeth poured everyone a glass of mango juice. There was an expectant silence. The condensation from Aisha's glass dripped slowly onto the table. Walter's eyes were on her encouragingly.

"I— has Walter told you about where my sister is?"

"No, dear," said Elizabeth. "The only thing we know is . . . well, you said she moved away."

"I wasn't going to tell something that wasn't mine to tell," said Walter.

"She fought with my mum." This felt like itching at new skin, the skin stinging with it. Walter's gaze was still on her. *Be brave.* "We haven't heard from her since. We're going to find her, we think she might be in Melaka . . ."

Aisha watched Elizabeth and Robert exchange a glance.

"Is Walter going with you?" Robert asked, his voice carefully neutral.

"Only if you come too," Aisha said, and replayed this in her head. She hastily amended it like a request: "I – we – would really like you to come. It would be so nice. I think – I think we really need your company. No pressure, of course, but we were hoping you would consider it . . . of course if it turns out she's not there, we'll go straight home . . ."

She looked down at her hands, trying to stop stumbling over her words. Saying it like that, it seemed even more ridiculous, asking these people to travel across the country with what little time they had left. Under the table, Walter squeezed her knee supportively, his fingers firm.

Elizabeth and Robert exchanged another glance. Robert quirked an eyebrow and Elizabeth gave a minuscule shrug of one slender shoulder. She got up to refill their glasses.

"Well that sounds great, Aisha," she said, setting the jug back down, sounding for all the world like an entire conversation had just passed between her and her husband.

Aisha said, surprised and on reflex, "Really?"

"We were planning to go for one last trip around the country anyway," Robert said. His thick eyebrows scrunched together kindly. "With one condition: we'll stop by a little place in Ipoh." He smiled at his wife.

Walter looked at them both, eyes bright.

Aisha heard his voice in her head: *They're great, for parents.* That fond tone of the offspring of a *happy* family.

"A little place in Ipoh?" Walter was asking. "You mean—"

"You've been there," Elizabeth said, brushing his hair out of his eyes. He sniffed and pressed it back down, grinning at her. "You probably don't remember."

"You were busy sucking on your toes for most of your time there," Robert agreed. "We don't expect you to remember much."

They turned towards Aisha, three anticipatory pairs of eyes awaiting her response.

"Well of course you don't have to," Walter said. He caught her gaze and held it. "We could go on our own and catch you up."

Aisha shook her head and smoothed out her skirt. She felt a little unfamiliar, a little out of place, a little taken aback by how easy it had all been, a little overwhelmingly grateful. "Ipoh sounds great," she said. She was sitting amidst all this kindness. She did not know if she could ever repay it.

Melaka: Where June Might Be
(a memory)

Aisha had said *Melaka* to Walter's family because it had been the first place that had come to mind when she had been leaking her anxious words all over their kitchen table. She had thought of Melaka because her mother's parents had lived there, in that town, her grandparents. Aisha barely had memories of them; they'd died before her father had gotten sick, really sick. June had been four years older; she'd remembered them well.

Sometimes June would lie in her bed and talk about Nek Dan and Nek Kah. Aisha would listen and make up the memories in her mind. Images of her grandparents would flicker in and out, elusive: the glint of gold of her grandmother's bracelet, or her grandfather's slight frown when he was reading the newspaper. Mostly she filled the memories in. The words would wind carefully up into the dark, float across the room to Aisha, and she'd try her best to fill the memories in.

June would talk about the house in Melaka, about visiting it during every holiday.

It was such a nice house, bigger than the one they had here, but so cosy and lovely, June would say. Wooden walls and vines creeping up them, always green and insistent and free. The house wasn't exactly small, but the backyard spread out magnificently: they had sturdy trees all around, and impatient cow grass everywhere, and it was barely cultivated, just a space in which wildness grew. Flowers and fruits and weeds, birds crying out sweetly and wild cats winding their way through the grass. There was even a little burbling stream in the back.

Inside there were so many pictures of us. June's voice

would run wistful. *And Nek Dan would feed me sweets and Nek Kah would let me read trashy novels and watch sinetrons.*

Aisha would sometimes think resentfully that she didn't care. She was greedy for the stories but she sometimes thought furiously about how much she didn't care, how could she care about two people she found it so hard to remember much about? She'd only had them until she was six, almost seven. June had had them for four whole years more. She'd had a whole two more people, when they had so few in their lives.

When their grandparents died, they had left their home to Esah, who hadn't used it. She'd found it too painful to go back, and left it in the care of a neighbour who loved the fruit the trees would bear.

June, though, had always been waiting to return, the next opportunity she could.

Packing

(the present)

Standing in the middle of everything she owned, Aisha didn't know what to bring with her. This was a trip with so many variables: what if they couldn't find June? How long would they spend looking? If they did find her, how long would they stay? Would she even let them in after three years of radio silence from her? Would she come back? Would her mother want her to?

What would her mother, physically faced with June, even begin to say? What could *Aisha* say?

This room hadn't only been hers, once. The faded pink sheets on the other bed had been stripped, and the bed itself was more a dumping ground for Aisha's clothes and things now, but it had been June's bed, once. It had smelled like vanilla and sounded like One Direction.

Aisha had talked to and laughed with and lived next to someone else for so long.

Long before this house, even. Long before this little house with the lime green door. There had been the first home, the family house, the one in Kuching where June had been born and then Aisha, where they had spent the first years of their lives. All Aisha's strongest memories from that house in Kuching were ones of mourning, of slow painful goodbyes, but June had still always been a presence in the night, a teller of tales, a hub of boyband music.

Aisha got up.

She packed a small suitcase full of clothes, added her stuffed elephant to her backpack, and threw and tucked in books, letters, precious old gifts where they could fit. Just in case they weren't coming back.

Hidden deep in the closet were the faded pink sheets. Aisha had stripped them off the bed one day and stuffed them in there. It seemed strange that June had left them behind, so beloved as they had been. Maybe pink had been her form of expression in the little house where Esah had been so careful with her daughters, and once she'd gone into the world she'd stopped having to express herself in only one way. Or maybe she was leaving behind a sign: *please remember me.*

The old wound itched. If June had wanted to be remembered so much, she could have returned.

Aisha packed the sheets anyway before she could change her mind, and then she zipped up her bag very hastily. She stood there staring at it. A packed bag looked so final.

Fleabag sauntered into the room and wound himself around her legs.

"Get off, please," Aisha said, detangling her feet from his absurdly soft, furry body, and flouncing herself down onto the bed, cross-legged. "You haven't been bathed. Didn't I tell you you weren't allowed upstairs?"

Fleabag took this information in while studying her intently. Then he gathered himself up and leaped onto the bed next to her. He batted his head at her thigh.

"You're so dirty," Aisha said, sniffing and refusing to oblige him. Up close, though, she could see the scar on his head where his ear had been. She wondered if it itched sometimes. Aisha knew how scars could itch. Maybe that explained the violent batting at her thigh.

Aisha scooped him up by the belly. He made a long, upside down U, and his meowing increased in longing and intensity.

"Get off my bed," she said. Here she could see the large furless patch on his leg. "Did you get into a fight, Fleabag?" she asked, setting him down on the floor. "Was it worth it?" He'd been out into the world, then. Maybe further than she'd ever been. "Was it over a girl? Was it over some territory you needed to claim?"

"Mew," said Fleabag, bracing himself to jump again.

"Don't you dare," said Aisha, shaking a finger.

"Mew," said Fleabag sadly.

"And don't you pee on the floor either," said Aisha. "I know Mak set out a makeshift litter thingy for you."

Fleabag asked, "Miaow?"

"No," said Aisha. "You can't come. You're a street cat and you'll probably get motion sickness and throw up all over the vehicle."

Fleabag looked like vomit already, that awful off-putting orange colour. Aisha refrained to mention this last part. There were some limits to rudeness, even to intruding felines.

"Mee . . . ow," argued Fleabag.

"I don't know where you'll go," Aisha said. "Don't ask me. You made it out there for so long, you obviously won't starve."

Walter's voice had been anxious when he'd said *I don't want it to be alone when . . .*

"Ugh," Aisha said. "I'm going to sleep."

There was a soft rustling noise when Fleabag landed on her sheets and curled up on her legs, a warm heavy weight.

"Oh would you not," Aisha said, but she didn't push him off.

A Dream, Part One
(dreamtime)

In Aisha's dream it was a sunny day.

She was in a strange room that seemed too familiar for a room she had never seen before. The walls were an off-white and there were Polaroids adorning a corkboard on one of them. In the corner there was a tiny closet and against an off-white wall there was a rickety-looking bed, and pushed against the rickety bed there sat an ancient-looking wooden desk.

When Aisha tried to approach the Polaroids on the wall, to see the faces on the little squares, they seemed to blur before her eyes.

She approached the open window instead. Outside, there were voices drifting up into the hot day, little drifting fragments of conversations she strained to catch. The voices all sounded cheery and untroubled. When Aisha leaned forward their owners were too far below for her to make out what they looked like.

The phone rang. It had come from a corded phone, one that was sitting on the ancient desk. When she picked it up June said without preamble, "Hello? When can I come and visit?"

"Visit?" Aisha said, confused. "But you live here." When she looked up again the walls were pink. The sheets on the bed were pink, and Aisha said to June, "*I* don't live here."

Voice staticky through the phone, it was Uncle Amin who answered. He said, "Well let's go then, what are you waiting for? It's Friday."

In one of those uncomplicated twists of dreams Aisha exited the room to find herself on the swing hanging from the heavy tree near the river, near their old beloved

Kuching house. She was flying through the air, exhilarated with it.

The river was lapping at the banks, murky and calm, and the sun was setting over the low hum of the city. Like this, just like this, for a fleeting second, Aisha felt without doubt that she was home.

"Higher?" Uncle Amin asked, and when she said "yes" he obliged, strong warm hands on her back, pushing her towards the sky.

Aisha cut an arc through the cool evening and thought she'd never been this happy. Turning to look at him, to share this joy with him, she found his face blurry, like one of the Polaroids in the off-white room.

Penang, and the Little House with the Lime Green Door

(nine to eleven years ago)

Nek Kah had had a fall first and died, and then Nek Dan had – well, he hadn't *had* anything. There had been no long illness, no sudden sickness. The distant relatives cooed melancholic things about how when a wife goes, her husband soon follows, but Aisha thought that had been such an abstract romantical notion, could you die just from being *sad*?

All June had said was that their grandfather hadn't been the same. She said he'd stared into the distance a lot and when he'd looked at you, he'd looked right through you.

They'd buried them within three weeks of each other. Then Esah had packed up most of the things from her parents' house in Melaka with the wildness in the back, and they'd flown back to their home in Kuching.

Kuching was where Aisha's parents were born, where they had gotten married, where they had spent a decade and more in love. It was where their children had been born and where they planned to spend the rest of their lives. In Kuching, sunsets were endless and the hours felt lazy and luxuriant, the roads wide and winding. The people walked slow, the days ran long, and the food was hot and wondrous. If you took a wrong turn and just kept driving, eventually you would come across sand. If you'd taken a right turn instead and just kept driving, eventually you'd come across jungle. It was a town that had stumbled its way into a city and was rolling with it, spreading itself out and growing into home for people who flew in, looking for one.

Kuching was *kolo mee* in the morning and sitting out in plastic chairs at night with friends. It was old wooden family homes and fresh new *kopitiams*. Aisha's earliest memories of *anything* – of school, of cycling, of June murmuring across the space between their beds and Pak tucking her into bed with a story – they were all formed in this place, this hometown of hers.

Their father, that great soft brown bear of a man, came to meet them at the airport when they'd flown back after their grandparents' funerals – he'd flown back early – and yet as he hugged them each tight, his face was troubled, lines around his mouth that hadn't been there before. In the car on the way home Esah was sitting in front, Aisha was drifting off to sleep and June was already snoring. It had been a long couple of weeks, filled with tears and exhaustion, deciding where her mother's parents would lie eternally.

And now Esah was asking, "What's wrong, Arif?"

And her father was saying, "Not now, *sayang*. We'll talk later."

And her mak was saying, desperate to hear and desperate not to know, "I know something's wrong, I can take it. Just tell me. I can take it."

And her father was darting his eyes to the rear-view mirror – Aisha's eyes squinted with almost-sleep – and answering quietly, "I got the results back."

After his brother Amin had died, long and drawn-out, Arif had put off the testing for as long as he could. He'd finally gone after Esah's mother had had the fall.

Esah sounded like she could not breathe. She was gasping in the car, but very quietly, because she thought her children were asleep.

There were two years in between this and the end. These two years Aisha found very hard to recall, not because she'd been too young, but because they were difficult to think about and difficult to remember: Arif's fat and muscle leeching away to haggard features and hollow bone. He did not have enough strength to hug any of them tight, at the end, and his voice was too hoarse for stories because of the tubes they kept sticking down his throat.

At nine she lost her father, her bearded bear of a father who bundled them up and stared at her mother with stars in his eyes and was the first teller of tales, a tradition June had continued after he had gone. When they buried him that heavily overcast day, Esah was very thin and very brittle. She had lost her parents and husband in the span of three years. She had no brothers and sisters, and the cooing distant relatives were scattered all over the country.

So Esah packed up their stuff and moved them to Penang. There was work there and what was most important was that it was far away from Kuching, across the country.

June said, "What about my friends?"

June had been thirteen and she had had many friends. She also had teachers she loved and little parts of Kuching that had been hers to explore. She had a favourite *ais kacang* shop and a favourite *cucur* stall. She had solid house walls that were familiar to her when everything else was falling apart. It was her father's city. He had raised her here. She stared at her mother, heartbroken and unwilling.

Aisha stared at the floor, at her feet, and wanted her father back. He would have done something. He would have ruffled June's hair, talked Esah down, and calmly fixed it all.

Esah said, "I can't stay here." She looked blankly about the house she had wanted to spend the rest of her life in. It was her husband's city, the city he had lived in and lived so well in. It was the end of the discussion.

A few months later, they stepped out of the taxi and stared at the little house in Penang, just before Aisha turned ten. It was two storeys and rather square, rather plain, like a child's drawing of a house. The walls were a soft blue and the front door was a bright lime green. There was a little patch of dry, browning grass in front. Wire netting knotted itself rather meanderingly about the house, a placeholder for a fence.

Aisha felt like crying, so she stuck her thumb in her mouth, a habit she'd long broken. June slid fingers through the fingers of her other hand, and tugged her forward.

Esah stayed in place, staring fixedly at it. "I can't," she'd said. "Oh, I can't do it."

"*We* can," June had said, turning around and not letting go of Aisha's hand. There was something indescribable in her expression. She did not seem like the June who Aisha had fought with and listened eagerly to all her life, who had begged her mother not to come here and cried quietly the whole flight to Penang. She now seemed suddenly older, and Aisha did not know how it had happened.

June said, "We're with you. One step at a time. Come on." With her other hand she tugged gently at her mother's sleeve. "It'll be okay, you'll see."

Their mother stared at her like she didn't recognise her either. June coaxed her through that one step, that first step, and the second. She pushed the wire netting that passed for a gate forwards and they stepped into their little house, June's shockingly pink suitcase trailing behind them.

Packing, and the Little Home with the Lime Green Door

(the present)

Aisha clattered down the next morning to find Esah at the kitchen table. Boxes lay around her mother, flaps open, some taped tightly closed with masking tape already. Aisha thought of the first day in the little house.

June had been loud that first day, even obnoxious. She'd teased Aisha and asked questions at Esah about things she hadn't needed to ask questions about. Esah had been irritated and brittle, but not very sad, because June had been a whirlwind, rushing through the rooms and leaving doors open.

"Does this go here?" she called over to Esah, balancing their mortar and pestle on the edge of the sink. It looked precarious.

"Be careful," their mother warned. "If that falls on your sister's foot— June!"

Esah and June had both tried so hard in their own way. Esah had been so cold and blank, after everything. On the plane to Penang she'd stared out of the window and sometimes it felt like she hadn't stopped since. She'd been so careful with Aisha, strict with June in a way she'd never been before. Aisha hadn't been allowed to go out alone to the park because Penang was unfamiliar. June had been forbidden to go on jungle climbing trips with friends because who knew what could happen. June was snapped at when she was fifteen minutes later than she'd said she'd be. Aisha told her teacher she couldn't attend a spelling bee a couple of states over. They looked at their mother, sitting alone in the kitchen and staring at her hands, and they didn't argue with what she told them.

And June had tried so hard, but she had been thirteen. In six years she would say *I've had enough of this house.*

Now the boxes lay scattered on the floor, on the kitchen surfaces. Esah rubbed her finger absently over the gouge in the wooden table and asked Aisha, "Is the cat coming?"

"Fleabag?" said Aisha. "Oh, I suppose."

Esah smiled. "I guess Walter would like that."

Aisha said, "Well. He gets what he wants." She was talking about both the cat and the boy. She stretched some tape over a box, revelling at the tearing, violent sound, and peeked inside: mostly mugs and bowls and plates.

"What's all this?" she asked after looking into a few more boxes, containing what looked like the contents of their whole house.

"I'm just," said Esah. She looked absently down at the boxes. "Just getting ready. I don't want – you know, if we don't have time, I'd rather have this house packed and . . ." She nodded unseeingly down at everything they owned.

"Well, I don't want to leave it just like that. In case it gets dusty. Just in case."

"Just in case," Aisha repeated. She watched her mother fiddle with the tail of her *tudung*.

"Do you think we'll come back?" Esah asked, still staring down at the bags and boxes.

Aisha almost said *Don't bet on it*. Death was intertwined with moving, in her head, with boxes and long trips across the country. This seemed appropriate, given the circumstances.

"This was a good home," she said instead.

Her mother said, "I don't know. I think sometimes it wasn't. I know sometimes that was my fault."

When Aisha looked up at her, her mother was looking back. Aisha didn't quite know how to interpret the expression on her face; regret, perhaps, or remembrance. A long, tremulous moment held.

They heard a honk outside.

The Campervan
(the beginning)

In the kitchen, Esah's duffel bag seemed heavier than it should be. Aisha set it down, breathing heavily, and unzipped it a little to peek inside. A lifetime's worth of recipes peeked back at her, written on notebooks and the pages of heavy cookbooks.

"Do you plan on cooking much this road trip, Mak?"

"Don't be smart," said Esah. "I am not risking leaving them behind." She flipped the tail of her *tudung* behind her shoulder, opened the door, and started rolling her suitcase down the little patch of grass. Aisha began following her.

Walter tumbled out of the campervan.

Aisha blinked as her eyes adjusted to the sun.

The campervan was a florid, sickly green. What appeared to be illustrations of red tentacles flung themselves all about it. Two wide anime eyes had been painted on top of its headlights. It was an explosion of a van, more than an actual one.

"Interesting choice of vehicle," Aisha said, as Walter hurried to help them with the bags.

"We got it cheap," Walter said, hoisting the duffel bag onto his back and smiling up at her. "My dad bought it off an old friend."

Aisha didn't ask if the old friend was into some sketchy Japanese subcultures. Walter's parents came out of the campervan next, waving at her.

Elizabeth said, "Esah, let me help you with that!"

"Please don't, Auntie," Aisha said. "There are rocks inside. At least that's how it feels."

"Cooking books," Esah amended. "I couldn't leave

70

them behind," she added to Elizabeth, who tutted sympathetically and said, "I know *exactly* what you mean."

They stepped up into the campervan, one by one, and looked around. Inside it looked chaotic and cosy all at once. There was a very nice sofa area with a pull-out bed, patterned with green, tentacled pillows. There was a little door to what Aisha assumed was the bathroom, and there was a kitchen area with a microwave, surfaces overflowing with fruit: mangoes, apples, bananas, oranges, rambutans.

"Ma doesn't seem to realise it'll take a day at most," Walter said apologetically. "Actually, both my parents have not realised that this will take a day at most." He waved a hand at the campervan in general.

"We can never have enough fruits," Esah said reproachfully. She and Elizabeth shared a tutting glance. *Children,* it seemed to say. *Think they know so much.*

"And we can never have enough space. Also we might as well travel in comfort," Robert said. "*And* we took all three juice squeezers! So we're set."

"Blenders, darling," said Elizabeth.

Walter unloaded Aisha's suitcase onto a little cupboard area and said, "Is that it?"

"I wish," Aisha said. Just then there was a loud *meow* illustrating this sentiment. She sighed and turned around.

"Fleabag!" Walter said, looking delighted. Fleabag had trotted out into the sun and was now at the door of the campervan, looking displeased at having been momentarily overlooked. He sat and lifted his bald leg to lick at it regally.

"Come on, buddy," Walter said, picking him up lovingly and bringing him in, pressing his fur against his cheek.

"This is our last chance to not get fleas," Aisha said.

Elizabeth looked slightly alarmed, but Walter said, "Don't be silly, Sha," to her and, "Look, he's perfectly clean, he licks himself all the time," to his mum. He took Fleabag to the sofa area, where he deposited him carefully down onto the luridly patterned pillows.

Fleabag looked suspiciously around at everything.

"You won't think I'm silly when he's vomiting all over the place," Aisha said to unheeding ears. "He seems like just the type to be carsick."

Robert shut the door and asked who wanted to drive first. Walter was cooing to Fleabag, Elizabeth was showing Esah her stack of mangosteens, so Aisha made eye contact with him, about to tell him she would.

Robert shrugged at her and tilted his head at everyone else, like they were in on a joke. "Thank you to everyone for volunteering so enthusiastically! I'll take the first shift," he said, winking, and made his way to the front.

The campervan moved with a lurch and Fleabag yowled. From the window Aisha watched the little house get littler and littler.

This was where she'd grown up. Esah was busy with Elizabeth, so she wasn't watching. But Aisha watched it shrink. *Do you think we'll come back? Just in case.* Just in case, just in case. This was where she'd grown up, for better or for worse. It had been *her* little home for so long when

73

Kuching couldn't be. June had left and Esah probably did not consider it home.

But Aisha watched it long and unblinking, something aching within her sternum; she watched it until she couldn't see the lime green of the door any longer.

Esah and Elizabeth and Robert

(two years ago)

When Esah had first met Walter's parents, she had been slightly wary.

"They're really good people," Aisha said. She sounded like an echo of Walter. "They'll love you."

"Even if they do . . ." her mother had said. She had not had to finish the sentence. Things like this came with too much baggage for it to be as simple as *They'll love you,* and both Esah and Aisha knew it.

"Well, they love me," Aisha offered.

Esah looked over and smiled at her, wry. Then she had looked in the rear-view mirror, making sure the curve of her *tudung* was even. They had gotten out of the car and waited at the gate of the large compound.

Walter came out with his parents. When he saw them he said, "Auntie!" as if this was the highlight of his day. He looked surprised when he realised it was raining and ducked back in to grab an umbrella. Esah relaxed fractionally at Aisha's side.

Elizabeth Jelani was in a red sundress. She said, "Come in, come in, it's pouring out there!"

Robert Gan came out with a large umbrella, and Esah and Aisha ducked under it, on either side of him.

"Cats and dogs out here," he said, on their rush back, and it didn't sound like just something to say to fill in the silence, coming from him. He was the kind of person who could pull it off.

When they were at the front step, Elizabeth handed a multitude of towels over to them and tutted sympathetically some more over the weather. She led them in and they all congregated in the living room, Aisha and her mother on one sofa, Elizabeth and Robert on the other, Walter on the piano seat looking between them sort of anxiously, sort of very slightly amused. Esah looked around at the photos of Walter on every available surface. She looked at Elizabeth and Robert and smiled.

There were a few moments of silence.

Elizabeth asked, "Are you hungry?"

"No, they just ate lunch," Walter said, just as Aisha opened her mouth to say yes just for something to do. Noticing this too late, Walter mouthed *Sorry* at her exaggeratedly, shrugging. She shook her head slightly, feeling some of her own tension dissipate at his amusement.

"We have some cakes," Elizabeth continued valiantly. "Or do you like mango juice?"

Esah, who was fastidious about fruit, said immediately, "Only if it's the Queenie kind," and Elizabeth's eyes had lit up.

"Your mother has taste," she said to Aisha, standing up and leading them to the kitchen.

Esah looked around at the clean kitchen, smiled at more photos of Walter on the wall. "Is that a Smeg?" she asked Elizabeth, indicating the blender nearest her.

"Do you have one?" asked Elizabeth, excited.

"Oh, I want one," Esah said, looking at it longingly.

"I've been meaning to work it," Elizabeth exclaimed, excited. "You can be the first one to try it out."

Aisha was thinking about this now, remembering how worried they'd been, watching her mother and Elizabeth's heads bent over the table. There had been nothing to worry about, it seemed. Only a few things mattered in the end. Only things that were really important. Things like mango juice, and the love of one's children.

On the Road

(the present)

Esah and Elizabeth were still sitting in the kitchen area, discussing something that sounded like carrot varieties, and so Walter and Aisha sat on what passed as a sofa. It was quite soft and sank comfortably under their weight, but the pillows were distracting. Aisha turned one of them over. The same pattern grimaced terribly up at her, lurid.

Fleabag rested in the patch of sunlight between them, purring occasionally as Walter stroked him.

Aisha watched the gentle repetitive motion, how considerate he was of avoiding the spots that made Fleabag nip, like the bald leg and the exposed stomach. Walter had such sure hands. He had clean, blunt nails, and thumbs that were slightly overlong. Like this, just like this, all the lines of his body were limned in the morning light.

Aisha longed silently to run her fingers over them.

"How do you really feel about this?" she asked quietly, tamping down the yearning.

"If he vomits I'll clean it up, I promise," Walter said, squinting fondly down at the ridiculous cat, who stared emotionlessly back at him.

"Not the cat. All of this," said Aisha. "I mean all of *this*." Walter looked up at her in time to see her gesture vaguely at the campervan, the trip, the long-missing sister. "I know we didn't really get a chance to talk about it properly."

Walter gave the question some consideration, his petting slowing. Fleabag took this opportunity to bat at him with one paw, but Walter just continued to stroke him, looking into the distance like he was really thinking about it. "How do I really feel? I'm excited," he said eventually. "I think it's exciting." He nodded, like he had made up his mind about something, his dark hair falling over his forehead and his eyes a lighter brown in the sun, almost golden. "You know, I thought perhaps we wouldn't get to go on a trip before . . . well, before. And that would have been sad."

Aisha watched him and Fleabag a bit more. She wondered how things could be so easy with him. He took time to make his mind up, but he always knew what he felt: unsure, upset, ecstatic. Aisha thought that she didn't really understand what she was feeling sometimes, like sometimes there was an ache that threatened to coalesce into a storm and she had no idea why.

She said, "Walter—"

She faltered, and tried again, biting the words out, low so her mother wouldn't hear. "What if we don't find her?"

"We will," Walter said assuredly, without any hesitation.

For some reason this abruptly irritated Aisha, which felt better than the slow ache. He didn't *know* that, and yet he was so sure. Sure when he was sure of so little in his life. "You don't know that," she insisted. There were a million places June could be. She might not even be on this continent, and there was no way of contacting her. She hadn't exactly left a number. She hadn't wanted to see them again.

"Have faith," said Walter. "You have a good idea of where she is, and we won't give up if it's not the right place." He shrugged gently at her.

Everything about him was gentle: the shrug, his eyes, the way he was petting that grumpy flea-ridden stray who clearly hated him and the world.

"I'm not going to believe in something if it's likely to disappoint," Aisha said shortly. "We *should* give up if we don't find her there. We can't just keep wasting your parents' time."

Walter looked at her, saw something in her face, and just said, "Okay." He looked away and down; he continued his stroking.

This calm was no help. No help with Aisha, no help with the journey. Walter was always too kind and too understanding these days until he was properly riled up. Aisha wished he was more riled up, she wished he would be snappy and sarcastic like he'd been before, she wished—

She had no idea what she was wishing for. Why would she be wishing for him to be *angry*, to be *aching*, to have a storm within him too? It was selfishness. The thought of selfishness just made her more irritable. There was a long road ahead and she wasn't sure if June lay at the end of it.

She said, "Stop petting that cat. It's going to be spoiled."

"I want to spoil him," said Walter, in a controlled, patient sort of way, without looking up again.

"It's no use getting attached," said Aisha meanly.

"I'd argue that there's plenty use," Walter suggested.

"Don't waste it on a cat!"

"There's not a limit to getting attached," Walter said. He sounded, finally, a little curt, and he still wasn't looking at her.

Aisha felt a little terrible. This sort of snappishness, this boundless irritability, it hadn't happened before. It was just that now there was a need to— but to what? She didn't know. There was nothing about Walter that had changed. So what was it that caused this constant hot combativeness that flared up so abruptly?

Looking out the window, she saw they weren't heading for the highway. Instead they were driving down a road Aisha remembered well: one that led to the Penang bridge. She could see it rising in the distance, tall and stately, and below the calm blueish water sparkling in the sunlight.

"Where are we going?" she said, distracted enough to forget that they had been on the cusp of an argument.

Walter still wasn't meeting her eyes. He'd stopped touching Fleabag. Aisha wished he hadn't.

"I asked my dad to make a pit stop."

The sea grew and grew. At the end of the world it would rise up in a tsunami but for now it just lay, placid and calm and bright. The towers on the bridge rose and rose, looking steady.

"We're going to the beach," Aisha said. "Our beach."

"Unless you don't want to." Walter sounded very neutral, seemed a chasm away, still looking down, his gaze fixed on Fleabag's ugly curry-fur. His face was expressionless.

Aisha didn't know why it was suddenly so hard to reach over and touch the sunlit curve of his shoulder. She longed to do it. She couldn't do it.

"I do want to," she said. "Of course I do."

Walter shrugged, a short movement, and he didn't say anything as the campervan rode smoothly over the long bridge.

The Beach, Part One
(four months ago)

It had been such a lovely day.

Their results had just come out a week ago. They'd met their conditional offers, somehow, incredibly, one way or the other, and they were going to university.

They were going to university.

The rest of their lives had been spread out so wide in front of them, and the road had been too, the bridge rising up to meet them, its towers tall and solid.

Walter had turned up at the little house that morning. He had texted *Come out,* and when she had, he had said, "Come on," and Aisha had taken his hand and climbed into the car, air conditioning blasting a welcome respite from the hot hot *hot* sun. They'd driven down roads, blasted the best of the 80s, and debated at length about where they were going to get lunch. Walter had been wearing a green Yoda shirt and sunglasses which hid his brown eyes, but Aisha knew they would be an amber brown in this light. She knew they were bright, the way they got when he was arguing for something passionately, in this case a proper lunch.

Phil Collins sang something about not hurrying love. Aisha, thinking about the way Walter squinted when he smiled, felt overwhelmed with it, even as Walter started on his eighteenth minute of discussing the merits of sushi versus *nasi campur* for the coming meal.

"We can have *char kuey teow*," she suggested eventually, resigning herself to his yelp of indignation at her adding another option. She tousled a hand through his soft hair as he parked at the beach's parking lot. She felt for his fingers with that same hand, slipped it into his, and they walked as the gravel turned into branch-strewn dirt into softer sand into real beach sand, damp and coarse and gritty. There were other people there, enjoying the long weekend. Families slathered in sunscreen with their kids shrieking happiness at their misshapen sandcastles; lazy groups of friends lying on bath towels and dozing off, water lapping gently at their feet; swimmers striking out wide and deep into the water.

The ocean spread itself wide and endless as far as the eye could see. The tide came in, came out, came in again.

Aisha had a large floppy-brimmed sunhat jammed onto her head. Her sweat-damp hair stuck thickly to her neck and clung. Walter had his sunglasses on and held a picnic basket in his other hand. He looked at the sun, that warm big ball of light, and mumbled something about melting.

Aisha watched a trickle of sweat make its considering way down the clean line of his neck, before disappearing into the collar of his t-shirt. She was struck with the sudden urge to reach out and follow it with her thumb.

"I was lying before," Walter announced. "I brought lunch."

"You made me listen to all that for nothing?" she demanded.

"I wanted to surprise you." He shrugged, the corner of his mouth curling up in a shit-eating grin. "We could have *nasi campur* for dinner."

Aisha mock pouted. "So I'm not going to get my *char kuey teow*?"

"No, but this is better," Walter promised reassuringly. They found a spot slightly further away from the crowd, near the big rocks, and he set the basket down, opened it, spread a large beach towel out. Apples came out next, then egg sandwiches, and two packets of *kolo mee*—

"Where did you get that?" Aisha asked. *Kolo mee* was a dish native to Kuching, rare in this part of the country; it was a delicious marvellous delicacy of oiled-up beef noodles, and Aisha missed it deeply and daily.

"I have my sources," Walter said, being as mysterious as he could while sweating profusely in the heat and carefully taking out a flask of what was probably juice, courtesy of Elizabeth's garden.

Aisha contemplated his flushed, damp skin, his sure hands around the cool condensation of the flask. "You're kind of wonderful sometimes," she declared.

Walter shrugged modestly, smiling a bit, but he looked pleased. He poured the orange juice into two paper cups and he said, "To university! And finally deciding what to do in university. Well, you have. I still might change it. Do you think I should, Sha? I mean I could email them, right? Remind me to later, I—"

The world was so wide-open, Aisha was almost scared to think of it. For so long there had been the scent of death that had haunted the little house, and Esah's brittle carefulness, manifesting itself in strict rule. In university a new life would begin. She would meet new people, live in new places, visit Walter on weekends and see the world. She would not be suffocated by grief, and she felt guilty with how good that thought was.

She didn't want to leave her mother but the world was waiting. Perhaps this was what June must have felt before she left. And unlike June, she would come back home sometimes, and she felt pretty good about that too.

She drank to it. As they watched, the tide came in, came out, and then it came in again. Like the day, it was endless.

They sat in the sand and built a fort, Walter scooping sand out of its moat again and again as water flooded in endlessly. Their laughter rose into the sea-spray, mingled with everyone else's, and was swallowed by the waves.

Walter said, "Pass me a Magnum," and Aisha realised the cooler hadn't been properly closed, and he was pouring the mushy ice into his mouth, reaching forward to touch it to Aisha's cheek as she laughingly batted him away . . .

And then the shouting started. Aisha looked around, startled. She didn't think of anything as big as tsunamis at first, she thought *heart attack. Broken leg. Someone drowning.* More people started screaming, their voices caught up in a sort of shrieking off-pitch chorus of grief, and then she thought *bombing, financial collapse, mass shooting*. She reached out her hand to Walter, who was starting to rise, eyes on the rest of the beach. Without looking at her he folded it into his. People had started getting up, kids in tow, picnic blankets left behind. The voices were dying away.

"We should go back," Walter said quietly. People were leaving the sand as quickly as the tide was coming in. They could have asked someone what was going on, but they didn't. They lifted the cooler and walked hand in hand to the car. As if honouring some silent agreement they'd made Walter had reached out and turned the car's radio off as soon as the engine rumbled on. David Bowie was cut off as he started singing about Planet Earth being blue.

The day did not feel endless any more. The world was closing in on Aisha.

Esah met them at the lime green door, her face pale.

The Beach, Part Two
(the present)

In the parking lot, Robert locked the campervan. Standing outside it, up close, it was more terrible-looking than ever, red and green in an almost menacing way, tentacles reaching out. Aisha turned away from it and nudged her knuckles at Walter's hand. It folded hers in itself without hesitation. Walter forgave easily.

Hand in hand they walked down the path. Now branches lay thickly in the way; this was evidently a job someone had stopped bothering with four months ago. Walter bent down once or twice to shift a particularly big one out of the way, until eventually the dirt gave in to soft soft sand, and then coarser, damper beach.

There were still a few families sitting on the sand. Their children's laughter was not high and shrieking like children's laughter usually was: maybe they could sense their parents looking at them and mourning all the years they would never grow old in. They were building sandcastles, though, building them tall. Every so often they would run to the sea to scoop some water for their castles, and run back to pour it intently into their moats. Their parents simply watched them silently, the expressions on their faces grave and attentive. They were committing this to memory. Every once in a while, they reached out to each other, holding on for comfort. Aisha knew what second-hand grief felt like. The seaside air was heavy with it.

She had to tear her gaze away. She did not feel she could think about this.

The sun caught and held on their skin, like it wanted to linger. Behind them, a short distance away, Robert and

Elizabeth and Esah followed down the twig-strewn path. Aisha wondered what they were looking at: the sea, the sky, or their children.

Robert said, "I haven't been here in some time." He stood and squinted into the horizon, and his gaze was far, far away.

Elizabeth linked her arm in his, the warm breeze drifting her straight soft hair into her face, and said quietly, "We used to take Walter here."

And Aisha could almost see what they were looking at, too: Walter at two, five, ten, his wide grin and chubby fists, making little forts and bringing his parents little pails of water. Elizabeth unfolding the picnic blanket and Robert resting comfortably on a brightly-striped towel, saying, "Yes, impressive work, son," very seriously at Walter's every sculpture.

Perhaps Aisha and Walter's first child would have looked like Walter as a boy. He would have been named Amin, not Arif, because for now her father's name still hurt too much to think about often. Maybe he would have inherited Walter's soft brown eyes and crooked canines, the way he listened and the way he loved.

Esah had brought them across the Penang bridge, down here during the school holidays. She had spent a long time looking absently over Aisha's shoulder and being jostled out of a reverie when Aisha had said, "Mak?" or pointed at a sandcastle she'd created. "Yes, well done," she had said vaguely each time, not really looking. Either that or she'd argued bitterly with June over what swimwear could or could not be worn to the beach, June rolling her eyes heavenward and clenching her fists. The first few years hadn't been great trips.

Then it had slowly gotten better, her long trances gradually shorter as time went by. They would still catch her by the kitchen window, but when interrupted she'd smile and ask if they were hungry. On the weekends she would still be lying in bed, on her side, breathing measuredly and evenly, but she would rise and ask about their day. She was still very careful with them: on beach trips she'd still fought with June about straying too far away from their spot on the beach and she had told Aisha firmly not to go into the water if it was higher than her waist, but she was there, more present than she'd been since Kuching. The trances had almost disappeared when June had left.

June had left.

Esah had not withdrawn again, exactly, but she had been a lot quieter after that. She was less strict with Aisha, as if trying to counterbalance what had made June leave. Aisha in turn spent a lot of time at home, very careful to not make her worry. She had not come back to the beach with her mother.

When Aisha had come later, with friends, then Walter, she determinedly had not thought about these trips.

Aisha knew Esah was remembering it too. Her mother was staring into the sea in a way Aisha was too familiar with.

"Mak," she said, the word feeling almost involuntary

in her throat. When her mother looked up, Aisha thought she would look right past her again.

But Esah just looked at her steadily, expression complicated, arms folded over herself, *tudung* tail catching in the slight breeze. She said, just loud enough that Aisha could hear, "*Alhamdulillah.*"

Aisha didn't know whether she was thankful for the sea, or the precious months left, or the chance of June.

They continued down to the shore, taking off their shoes along the way. Elizabeth gently set down a towel and she and Robert sat on the sand, but she set another one down for Esah, too. She started murmuring to her about the weather or the waves, Elizabeth was always kind like that, in quiet ways.

Aisha and Walter held hands right into the water. They did not say anything until the water was right up to her ankles, her knees, then her waist. Her mother did not shout out for them to be careful.

Aisha was in shorts and a T-shirt and she wasn't

dressed for the beach, but she didn't stop. The water was warm under the sun and they kept walking on, holding hands, gasping slightly at the shock and momentum of the cool waves coming in.

Aisha was looking at Walter, though, instead of the sea, instead of where they were heading. Walter's skin was damp from perspiration and so was his hair, curling a bit at the neck. His mouth was a little open and his brow a little furrowed. His brown eyes were fixed on the horizon.

Good. He could be a compass. He could tell them where to go.

Something inside Aisha burned white-hot, not just for the potential child they could have had who'd never go to a beach and build a fort with his chubby fists, but for everything else: the future that had been so nearly within grasp. Their child might have had bright eyes and maybe the exact shade of her brown skin, Walter's lovely large fists and smile, but he had always been a dream, still hypothetical even then, even now.

Aisha had had so many other things that had been very firmly on the horizon, so very clear and non-hypothetical. The apocalypse had been announced the day she'd gotten her results. She'd gotten the grades she needed for her first-choice uni. There had been a chance of a life without grief. The world had been so—!

They were chest-deep. They stopped. Aisha's toes curled into the soft wet sand below her. Each time a wave came in, she was momentarily weightless.

"Be nice to Fleabag," Walter said, finally turning. Finally looking at her.

"Walter," Aisha said, her chest hurting. Maybe it was the water pressure, she thought nonsensically, or maybe it was the endlessness of the sea's horizon.

"I know," said Walter, and held her hand.

Aisha wondered if he knew, what he knew, because it felt like she herself didn't.

"Walter," she said again, because it felt like it was important. But there were no words in her throat. A sense memory instead crept in, of that last day at the beach, Walter's hand folded firmly in hers, ready to face the news. Over the gear stick, over the screaming, holding tight. He seemed so distant, in the ocean next to her and somehow a million miles away.

He was still holding on tight.

Ipoh

(the present)

Fleabag flinched and ran away from them when they returned, dripping. Robert headed to the front, stretching and popping his joints in anticipation for the road ahead. Aisha grabbed some clothes and commandeered the bathroom to change. Walter went in next. Aisha, after flicking wet fingers at Fleabag to make him scowl, sat with him. He attempted to jump into her lap once more. Aisha let him, because she'd promised Walter to be nicer.

Up close, Fleabag wasn't quite so distastefully coloured – there were patches of brown and even gold mixed in with his stale-curry orange – but he still obnoxiously stretched in her lap, headbutting her hand for scritches.

"We're not quite there yet, all right," Aisha said. "Don't be presumptuous." She put her hand on his warm, breathing little body, but very firmly did not give into his demands.

The campervan meandered out of Penang, and Fleabag's weight *was* comfortable, in a distastefully coloured kind of way . . .

Esah and Elizabeth sat on the sofa, too, at the far end. Elizabeth was telling Esah where they were going. She was softly telling Esah about a little house, which seemed so strange . . .

Aisha drifted in and out of sleep, maybe, and she dreamed of their little house, coming home to their front door. The campervan rocked steadily on . . .

Once she woke up as it hit a bump and she found she'd been drooling a bit on Walter's shoulder. He had sat down next to her when she'd been napping. She rubbed the back of her hand hastily over her mouth and looked at him, but he was asleep too, his head rocking gently with the movements of the campervan. Tiredly, Aisha registered the comfort of him being right there, radiating warmth, all his familiar lines somehow softened in slumber. He was so very close.

If they had been alone, she would have reached out to touch. The curve of his jawline, perhaps, or the side of his neck. Anything to be closer.

Instead she looked out of the window and it was such a warm day. The roads had changed, shrinking into something a little less wide, and shopfronts hovered, little squares of colour barricading the street. Aisha wanted to keep her eyes open, to watch how the cityscape changed around her, but they were already fluttering shut again.

She woke up properly when Elizabeth said, "Walter, look."

Walter moved sleepily by her side, a solid breathing presence. He stirred languidly, the movement something very feline, and asked, "Where are we?"

Aisha rubbed at her eyes with a fist and peered out. They were parked in front of a little house. But this wasn't Penang any more, and the house didn't have a green door.

"This was your first home," Elizabeth said, halfway out the door already. Robert was waiting for her outside; she took his hand and stepped out.

Walter moved slowly to his feet and smiled at Aisha. "Sha, look at that, come and see," he said. They were in Ipoh, Robert and Elizabeth and Walter's first home, the one stop they'd needed to make.

They stepped out. Lit by early evening light, the house they were parked in front of had a faded FOR SALE sign on its gate. The gate had almost been taken over by winding, curling vines, and what looked like a tree was growing from the window of the first floor of the house, its branches stretching up into the air emptily. The house was two storeys tall and determined green climbers had taken the rest of its walls completely over, so it was hard to see much of the actual building. What was left of the paint was faded and flaking, a strange mismatch of browns and moss-greens and the remnants of what might have been a soft yellow. Robert and Elizabeth stared up at it like it was a castle.

"It's so strange, seeing it again," Elizabeth said in quiet awe. "We got married here. One ceremony in the longhouse, another here. This little house."

"Looks great, Ma," Walter said, squinting up at it, "really homey, shall we go in and see my old bedroom?" and she cuffed him about the head gently.

"You should have seen it on our wedding day," she said. "Freshly painted, so many people. Your dad was so pleased. We were so broke, but we'd made the down payment all by ourselves. Our savings."

"You should have seen it when we brought you back from the hospital for the first time," Robert said. "That was when it finally felt like a home."

"That was when it was a mess," said Elizabeth.

"That was when it finally felt like a home," Robert

repeated fondly, pulling her towards him. They stared up at it together, lost in their own memories.

Aisha looked at her mother, who was staring up at the window that contained the errant tree branches that reached out into the sky. When Aisha thought of home, she did not think of Kuching any more, but when Esah thought of home . . . Had their little house in Penang, which had been Aisha's home for nine years, ever felt like a home to her?

Or had it always been that first house in Kuching, where she'd first brought June home, then Aisha; where she had kissed Arif's hand and taken him for her husband as her parents had given her away; the house where he'd lived and he died. And he'd lived – oh, how well he'd lived, so well that everything that came after must have seemed a pale approximation of life to her mother. What happened when someone who made a home a home for you was not there to make it one any more?

"I don't remember it at all," Walter said wonderingly,

standing on the pavement and staring up at the same window. His toddler soles must have touched this pavement, and maybe he had fallen down on it, maybe he had propped himself up on chubby fists and bruised knees. The thought curled in Aisha like something unexpectedly precious.

"We moved when you were three."

"I wish I could remember some of it," Walter said, not looking at the house, but at his parents. Aisha understood this sentiment bone-deep.

Elizabeth shrugged. "We made other memories. It's fine if you don't." Her arm reached out to pull him in, and all three of them stared up at it. The house stood there, flaking and old, a whole building standing as a testament to the life they'd once had.

Had Aisha's mother made other memories? Or had all the good ones been formed before? Her parents, when they'd lived and loved her. Her wedding. Her years with Arif. What was what came after? Esah's forty-fourth birthday, one of Aisha's best memories with her – they'd baked messily, creating cakes all day. Aisha's graduation from secondary school where Esah had stood and cheered. June's first painting being sold and Esah squeezing her in pride.

Perhaps all she remembered of life post-Kuching were things she'd rather forget: June sneaking out later and later every year and Esah getting more and more exasperated with it, her voice getting sharper and sharper. Exhaustedly driving Aisha back from tuition and co-curricular activities and badminton practice alone. Walking the streets in a town she'd never planned to grow old in. Staring out of the window of a house that was never supposed to be her home.

It had been where Aisha had lived. It had been her life. Staring up at Walter's ruined, beautiful first home, she decided that feeling guilty about the fact was exhausting. She had grown up in Penang and most of her friends were there. She had teachers she loved and badminton in the evenings and a favourite hill to sit on and watch the evening turn gold.

They might have been the worst years of her mother's life. Maybe Esah was glad they might not ever return.

Aisha had so many memories of it, bad and good and everything in between. These memories were hers. It had been a home.

A Short Conversation

(the present)

Walter was reading *The Children of Húrin*; he'd been attempting to finish Tolkien's works as part of his bucket list. Walter's bucket list stretched several pages and included currently impossible things like mountaineering and deep-sea diving, but he ticked items steadily off it anyway.

Aisha, who stubbornly refused to talk about any bucket lists, was attempting to inspect Fleabag for lice properly. He squirmed in her hands, lifted high into the air, hind legs kicking.

Esah was saying, "Aisha had jaundice. She got all

yellow." She and Elizabeth were sitting at the kitchen table again.

Elizabeth smiled around a mug. "Walter was colicky. The way he would cry."

"Oh, the crying," said Esah. "I think at one point I bribed her all the money I owned to stop."

"They have no idea," Elizabeth said, shaking her head in Walter and Aisha's general direction.

"I was luckier than most," said Esah. "I had my mak to take over when it got bad. The number of times I called her, crying, just exhausted. She would come over and I'd just pass out on the sofa for hours."

"Oh, me too," said Elizabeth. "I called my indai up at midnight asking things like *is he sniffling too much?* Enda aku nemu, *listen to him, he's sniffling a bit too much.* For the next few minutes she'd have to listen to Walter breathing perfectly fine." Her voice was fond. She was dimpling, canines showing. "I wouldn't have made it without her." A pause. "I miss her every day. I mean, I still feel her, you know? Her spirit."

Esah, who had never said it to her children, had never explicitly expressed her grief as long as Aisha could remember, ever since they'd packed up and moved to the little house with the lime green door, said, "Me too. I miss her so much."

A little silence at the table. Esah took a quiet gulp of the mug she held.

"I named Walter after my grandfather, and it made my mother very happy," Elizabeth told her, sharing this as a gift.

"I named Aisha after my mother," Esah said. And then she said, "I named June because I liked the name."

Aisha had been absently petting Fleabag, listening to the conversation, but now she stilled. Fleabag sensed this opportunity and wriggled himself out of her grasp, landing heavily onto the floor with an "'eow". Esah didn't seem to notice him.

"It's a very pretty name," Elizabeth said gently, her tone just like her son's when she pitched it like that.

"She was a very pretty baby," Esah said after a moment, fingers clenched firm against the handle of her mug.

"I can believe it. You must show us pictures one day, you know," Elizabeth suggested, her tone still very kind.

Esah said quietly, "I did bring some."

Elizabeth nodded supportively. "People always said, oh why have them developed, but I never held with that," she said, encouraging. "I always said, photos are physical, they're lasting, you can bring them out and look at them, plus they'll be handed down for generations—"

She stopped abruptly at this.

Esah said, "*Oh*," the exclamation sounding inadvertent, and Walter put his book down. For a long moment nobody said anything.

Then a sharp noise that could have been amusement escaped Elizabeth's lips. "Well, handed down for eight more months, anyway." And then she said bitterly – Aisha had never heard her bitter – "We were carrying these babies longer than that."

Esah reached out and took her hand over the table. "Yes," she said.

The moment lasted, lingered, ached in immeasurable sorrow.

Elizabeth shook her head once, furious and sharp, and eventually Esah said, "Those were the most uncomfortable eighteen months of my life."

But she smiled and looked at Aisha. "The way you were pressing on my bladder. And my ankles! The back pain has never gone away, you know. I couldn't sleep, I couldn't sit . . ." She carried on airily this way for a few minutes, until Elizabeth lifted her head and said, "Walter induced false labour at least three times. I kept having to go to the hospital."

"All that trouble," Esah said. "Well, I guess we got a few good kids from it."

"They're okay I suppose," said Elizabeth, who believed in unconditional love but didn't believe in over-praise.

Walter announced, "Thanks for that, Ma!" and

accompanied it with a dramatic roll of his eyes, all for show. The line of his neck was still tense. Aisha wished she could squeeze his hand, but she seemed to be physically unable to reach over to do it.

Elizabeth smiled at Walter, and it looked slightly less watery. "You know," she said to Esah. "They'll do what they want. You can say what you want, but they will. At a point all you can do is support them."

After her first meeting with them, Esah had come over to Elizabeth and Robert's house several times to make juice. She had had Walter over often and they talked baking. In the end none of the other stuff mattered. They came from a country that had a history but they were making their own. They were trusting their children to make their own. They loved them more.

"That's parenting for you," Esah said. "They'll have different lives from you, and all you can do is be there." It sounded like they were talking about something else. Maybe a dozen other things. Perhaps a future that now might never be. Esah said *be there* a little uncertainly, a little unused to it, but perhaps it was just Aisha. Esah had been there, actually, all her life. She had been the most constant presence.

It was just unfortunate, Aisha figured, that much of that time she hadn't really been there at all.

Kuala Lumpur
(the present)

Kuala Lumpur had been a slick city of tall skyscrapers and community-based *kampungs*, of billboards and colonial architecture, of 'expatriates' living large in luxury apartments alongside 'immigrants' cramped in makeshift buildings. Traffic swarmed constantly, red and yellow car lights shining steadily on even late at night, while the city was constantly constructing and developing and moving forward.

The streets were empty now. Large buildings looked abandoned: some of them looked like they would welcome invading creepers up their walls for a little company. Most people were with their families, had travelled back home to different states or moved in together in houses where communities grew and bred and traded. 'Rent' did not apply any more, and so all these beautiful sleek apartment buildings were wasted.

Esah was driving now: she'd persuaded Robert to get some rest and he was lying on the pull-out bed, snoring gently.

"This is going to mess up your circadian rhythm, silly

man," Elizabeth said to his sleeping head. Sitting beside him, she had passed a gentle hand over his hair. It felt like such an intimate moment, Aisha had had to look away.

Walter was watching the window, so Aisha watched him instead, the set of his full mouth and the focused expression, as if he was trying to commit the city to memory. Outside, streetlights glowed faintly, but mostly it was a dark stretch of road. It was so strange seeing skyscrapers' dark silhouettes ranged against the city sky. Kuala Lumpur had been framed as a city of tourism and advancement and education and opportunity. To see it so silent you could not escape the fact that this was happening: real, final, and here. Aisha looked away. She looked away.

The headlights illuminated a large wide-open gate, and a sign that looked familiar.

"Mak, are we stopping at your uni?" Aisha asked.

Esah said, "I wanted to surprise you."

Elizabeth smiled at Aisha.

The headlights lit up a campus that looked more like

a little neighbourhood than anything: small driveways leading up to faculty buildings in between lots of green trees that were flourishing and large parks that looked dark and abandoned. Esah drove until she reached a sign in front of a faculty building that read *Fakulti Sastera dan Sains Social.* Then she stopped the campervan and said, "Come on."

"This seems like a horror movie's first scene," Aisha said, but she came out anyway. There were little streetlights still on along the driveway but mostly it was the headlights that lit up the front of the building.

Esah touched her fingers to the sign and said, "I met your father here. In this building."

"Pak?" Aisha repeated. She'd known they'd met at university, but she hadn't known where and when. She might have known more if he'd died a few years later. Up until he'd died she'd heard little scraps of stories of their early lives together, little inside jokes, but it hadn't occurred to her to ask; she had been too young. It hadn't occurred to her that her dad would have died and her mother would cleanse their lives of any and all stories of him, going cold and hollow and quiet.

But Esah was opening her mouth, and she was saying, "It was my first lecture," and she was staring up at the building as if she could see right through the walls and years, to 1983 and the lecture theatre inside. "And after he asked if any of it made sense to me, you know? I said it did and he should pay more attention next time if it hadn't to him." The side of her mouth quirked, a brief twitch that looked more like an echo of amusement than actual amusement.

Aisha was quiet. She was absolutely silent, because any noise might break the spell.

"I was going to be very focused, I said, before I came to uni. I wasn't going to let myself get distracted by any boy. But he was always there, and he was part of my friend group, and we ate lunch together and talked about lectures together and walked round the lake together and I couldn't help but get to know him. And once I got to know him . . . well. You know the rest."

122

Again Esah touched the sign. She was speaking without much emotion in her voice, very matter-of-fact, as if this wasn't the first real story she had told about Aisha's father for years. As if she dropped little tidbits of information about Pak every single day, little stories down in Aisha's lap, nonchalantly.

"I wanted to marry him. So I came back after the third year and told my parents, well he's coming to *merisik*. And they were laughing, like, you came home with a degree and a fiancé, women these days *can* have everything." She smiled properly then, with her whole mouth, lost in the memory.

Aisha barely dared to stir.

"Your father loved you very much, *sayang*," Esah said, still looking at the sign, still not looking at Aisha, still using that voice that was on the edges of casual. Aisha couldn't see her face. "I don't tell you enough."

The responses in Aisha's throat ranged from *I'm so sorry you had to lose that kind of love* to *You don't tell me anything,* and she did not know which response would escape her so she stayed silent. Her mother turned from the sign and hugged her, brief, tight, and stepped back to the campervan. Aisha still could not see her face.

"Enough of standing around looking at buildings," Esah said, brisk. "Let's get back on the road."

A Short Conversation
about Forgiveness
(the present)

They had the dinner Elizabeth and Esah had both packed from home (*ayam pansuh, pucuk paku,* and a lot of rice) sitting at the kitchen table, all of them tired, all of them contemplative.

Sometimes it felt unreal. All the time it felt unreal, actually, because after the moment you woke up, after the space between not-remembering and realising, how could you fully accept that reality? That it was all going, going, gone, everything you ever knew and everyone you ever loved?

Some people had gone mad with it, ripping all their clothes off and roaming the streets, unable to accept the end. Some people hadn't been able to accept the end, and made the end come quicker for themselves.

When Aisha thought about *acceptance* – which she tried not to do most of the time, and when she did it was always studiously in a very abstract, almost academic sort of way – she wondered mostly what her father had felt, facing his end. Would it have been this hard to believe? Would he have felt this numb? Or did the fact that the world he knew would go on turning, and the wife and children he loved would keep right on living, give him more comfort than what they all had to face now?

Aisha thought about it sometimes, distantly, but mostly she didn't, in the same way she didn't think about Walter's bucket list.

They finished dinner and Robert said, "Well. We've got two choices: continue driving now and arrive late at night, or call it a night and drive in the morning."

Walter and his family looked expectantly at Esah and Aisha.

"It'd be hard to find anything at night," Aisha said, in turn looking at her mother.

"And we're all tired, another long drive probably isn't the best idea." Esah looked at Robert's yawn, at the slightly dark circles under Elizabeth's eyes, and said, "You've been so kind. I don't know how I can ever repay you – *sikpat kamek*—"

"*Udah*," Elizabeth said dismissively. "Nothing to talk about except where we're all going to sleep."

In the end, they insisted she and Robert take the pull-out. Walter took the sofa, and Esah and Aisha took turns blowing the air mattress up. They pulled a blanket over themselves. Fleabag leaped onto the sofa to curl up next to Walter. Aisha could see his eyes shining in the dim light, watchful and gleaming and cattish.

"Goodnight, you," Walter said, soft. Aisha yearned to curl herself around him. She touched his dangling hand. In the dark it was easier to reach out.

"Goodnight," she said.

"It'll be okay," he said.

"You don't know that," she answered, but it had no bite. "Get some sleep," she said, just in case he thought otherwise.

"Yeah, okay, boss," Walter said, more an amused, tired exhale than anything else. Eventually she could hear his breathing even out. Eventually the gleam from Fleabag's eyes disappeared as well, as he went to stalk around the campervan or whatever it was he would do tonight.

Aisha's nap in the afternoon had been long enough that sleep did not come easy to her. She tried not to move, though, because the air mattress squeaked if she shifted. She heard it squeaking now. Her mother moved and moved again, warm and awake beside her, and she eventually murmured to Aisha, "Are you up?"

"Yes," Aisha said.

"Do you think your sister will forgive me?" Esah said, laying it there, stark and bare in the night. Something inside Aisha went still and stiff at this question that her mother had just laid out there in between them. As if Esah attempted this kind of conversation every day. As if she had not been silent about June leaving, just like she had been silent after their father had died. As if she had ever indicated in the last three years that she might have needed to be forgiven by June in any way.

Aisha's mother had gotten better, even before June had left, even after. Esah had talked to Aisha about cooking, about school, and Aisha no longer worried about coming home to her mother's empty stare. But she never talked about the people they'd lost. Aisha did not know what to say now. She was coming up empty and numb, because she really didn't want to think about this. She thought abstractly about how unfair it was for Esah to bring up something like this after all this time and expect Aisha to know what to say.

"I don't know," Aisha said, because she didn't. "How would I know?" She didn't know if June would forgive their mother. She didn't know if Esah had really done something that needed to be forgiven, or if it was June who had by walking away. She didn't know why it was only June who forgiveness was sought from, or if they would even be able to find her, or if she was still alive at all. Death and travelling across a country, in Aisha's mind, were all invariably connected; it stood to reason that they might even be too late to see June one last time.

"I don't know either," Esah said lowly.

In the dark Aisha searched for words that would help her mother feel better, but came up with nothing. She tried for some feeling other than intensely indifferent, but came up empty. It felt a little callous, a little guilt-inducing, and she suddenly felt very tired.

Her mother didn't say anything else. The last thing Aisha thought before she finally fell asleep was, *I might see my sister tomorrow.*

A Dream, Part Two
(dreamtime)

In Aisha's dream she was seven and at home, at *home*, at *home*. It was a birthday party and it was a big one, and there were balloons and streamers, and so much *kuih penyaram*, the deep-fried sweet goodness she loved. Walter was there and he was seven, too. He was sitting with her father and listening as Arif read him *Goodnight Moon*, which was a favourite of Aisha's and always had been. Seven-year-old Walter had familiar crooked canines and they were exposed because his mouth was open: he was listening very, very seriously.

Arif said, "Goodnight, room . . ." and Esah swooped into the room, carrying a big birthday cake.

June said, "Blow out the candles, Sha!" and she was twirling about the room in a lacey pink dress.

Aisha leaned down and blew and everyone clapped, and then Arif said happily, "Goodnight, kittens," and he looked curiously down at his hand, which was melting away into dripping wax.

Uncle Amin was there. He looked at his brother sadly but he couldn't reach out to help, looking at his own hand curiously as it leeched away into haggard flesh before his eyes.

Esah said, "Arif! *Iboh giya*, you're scaring them."

June twirled and twirled and was all skirt, less girl. More notion, less sister.

"Goodnight, stars," said Arif, and Aisha said, "No," because this wasn't right, and Arif said, "Goodnight, air," and the room wreathed itself in a thick black cloud of smoke.

The cracks started appearing in the floor, exposing hot red lava that boiled and bubbled like a pot on a fire. Aisha tried to save her birthday cake but it jumped itself into the cracks. Walter looked curiously at where it had gone, his face covered in soot, tears running down his cheeks even as his stare was inquisitive.

Melaka

(the present)

Aisha was only sobbing a little bit when she woke.

She scrubbed at her cheeks and headed straight for the bathroom.

When she came out she had no idea if the adults knew she'd been crying: they were all sitting on the sofa, discussing something which stopped as they looked up and smiled at her. It was early morning, cool sunlight streaming in, touching the silver in Robert's hair and catching the edges of Esah's brooch: they were all framed in it.

"There's sliced mango on the table!" called Elizabeth, and Aisha said, "Thank you, Auntie," politely.

She took the Tupperware with her as she went up to the front. Walter was commandeering the campervan like he handled most things: completely earnestly and capably, trying hard and usually succeeding in what he was doing. But he always drove a little too fast.

"You're driving a little too fast," Aisha offered, and snuck a mango slice into his mouth.

Walter chewed and swallowed and said, "I'm making use of the daylight we have left." It was eight a.m.

"Your mum's going to say something in a minute," Aisha said.

"Hrmph," Walter hrmphed quietly. The needle inched back to a more acceptable speed.

Aisha sat down in the front passenger seat and buckled her seatbelt conscientiously. She said, "I had a dream."

"Was I in it?" Walter asked.

"Yes," said Aisha.

"Nice," said Walter, grinning. "Always good to know you think of me."

She said, "It was a bad dream, don't get your hopes up."

Walter took his eyes off the road.

She said, "And don't take your eyes off the road."

"Are you okay?" asked Walter. "Do you want to talk about it?"

Aisha said, "Not right now," and Walter didn't seem surprised.

He just said, "If you do, I'm here."

"I know," said Aisha.

"I'm always here," Walter said.

"I know."

Elizabeth called out, "You're driving *much* too fast Walter Gan Kee Peng!"

The needle inched back a little more. They had already been driving for some time; Aisha wondered why she'd been oversleeping recently. These roads were roads she could almost remember, but didn't, but still felt so familiar, the way her grandparents' faces flickered. These roads narrowed back into roads that were difficult to navigate a campervan through; Walter's driving slowed significantly.

Melaka was a city of red buildings and church ruins. It was a city of large old schools and children kicking a muddy ball across large old fields. It was a city of rickety shopfronts and generations of those who had been born as sea-traders from all over the world wandered onto this strange new land and fell in love with the women on it. These children had been born with sea-song in their blood, and some of their fathers had left but most had stayed. There were children to be raised and history to remember, in this city. A river wound its way through it and it lapped at the heels of the people who lived there.

Melaka was small and old and full of memories and knew that these were three precious things about it.

Aisha felt something like panic crawling slowly up her sternum as they neared the city centre. She knew her grandparents' house was close, was near here, was a tangible place that wasn't just a possibility.

Walter said, "You'll have to navigate, I don't know where to go from here." He stopped the campervan by the road.

Aisha said, "I don't remember where the house is." This was all she could manage.

Walter looked at her, knowing more than he should, and was about to say something, but her mother's voice wound its way from the back.

It said, "I do." Esah came up to the front and repeated, "I do. It's okay. I remember," and sat down in front of the wheel. Of course she remembered. She had come back here countless times all her life. She had come here that last time and buried her parents.

Aisha thought then that her mother must remember so many places. They drove on and on, places she barely remembered, even dream-like, and yet Esah's hands and gaze were so sure.

The House with the Door

(very much the present)

Aisha knew it was the house before her mother stopped. It was just like in the stories June had told her. Wooden walls and vines winding their way up them, a deep, healthy, flourishing green. The vines didn't look wild the way the abandoned buildings did: someone was trimming them, tending to them, keeping them off the windows and the door. The space around the house, however, was significantly more uncultivated: a place where wildness grew. A mango tree curved its heavy branches over the gate; a rambutan tree hid half the house from view. In the distance, in the back, which stretched out behind

the house as far as the eye could see, Aisha thought she saw chilli plants, thought she smelled orchids, thought she heard birds crying out into the world above a little babbling stream.

Cow grass grew thickly before them; there was no path, but a way was trodden through the grass to the front door. The grass was fairly short, too: someone was mowing regularly.

Aisha remembered all of the stories June had told her, but she recognised it because of the front door.

The front door was a bright lime green.

The paint looked fresh, as if someone had carefully gone over it recently. It wasn't exactly the shade of the front door at home, but it was close.

Fleabag, who had made his way to the front of the campervan, jumped onto Aisha's lap and turned his furry head to the window, watching the door as if he knew this as well.

Esah seemed like she was frozen to her seat, her hands still on the steering wheel. She wasn't moving at all. Aisha touched her gently on her shoulder, picked the tail of her *tudung* up and draped it carefully behind her.

"Be brave," she said. She didn't say *for me*, because she didn't know if it mattered. *For June,* she could say. Or *for the end of the world.*

After a long moment Esah nodded.

The new skin Aisha had barely grown itched and itched. Instead of tending to it she placed a hand on the top of her mother's spine, just to let her know she was there.

June

(the present)

They made their way off the campervan. Fleabag followed close behind. Walter hovered, unsure, on the fringes of Aisha and Esah's periphery, until he settled for slightly behind Aisha. She could sense him there, a solid comfort, a warm presence. The gate creaked open and they stepped onto the grass path. Robert and Elizabeth trailed some distance behind them, giving them space.

Aisha stood beside her mother but did not look at her for fear that she'd lose her nerve. She did not hesitate when she reached the front door. There was no time for that. She steeled her nerve and numbed her sternum.

Then she lifted a fist and knocked on the door. Be brave.

She was half expecting no reply. She knocked a second time. Her mother was still, beside her. The bravery began to falter, replaced tricklingly with doubt. Did they think June, who'd wanted to do so many things in the world, would end up here? She was probably in Potosi or Uppsala, Busan or Geneva. She was halfway across the world. She had been attacked by someone half-crazed by the end of the world.

For a wild second, Aisha even considered the possibility that she must have gone back to the little house in Penang. She must have gone back, even as they had made their way here.

But the door swung open and there she was. June was there.

June was there. There she was.

She had dyed her whole head now, Aisha saw. Her hair was up in a bun and shockingly pink tendrils curled around her ears.

June had always been taller than Aisha, older than her, more eager to go and eat the whole world up, and Aisha had always been striving to catch up. Her big sister had Esah's short quick fingers, her wide hips, and her temper. And then there were the things Aisha realised she had almost forgotten about her father in the past three years: June had Arif's ears, too, charmingly sticking out, his deep voice, the way he was unfailingly kind to anything helpless.

It wasn't only June who'd opened the door. Aisha's gaze caught on some movement. Someone small was hiding behind her legs. The someone poked his dark head out and asked, "Who are *these* people, June?"

June didn't answer. She stared and stared and stared. The small someone pulled gently on her right trouser leg.

"June," Esah said, like an exhale. The name sounded rusty like that, disused and old, like the creaking of the gate.

"June," their mother said again, like she was practising the name, but still June said nothing, staring, her mouth gaping open in shock. Aisha had the uncharitable thought that there was a distinctly goldfishy look to her.

The small someone shifting to look out caught their attention again, making them look away from June. His young face looked inquisitive and suspicious, all at once.

"Is he yours?" Esah suddenly blurted out, her ability to count appearing to disappear at this moment of crisis. Aisha thought, almost hysterically, that of all the things she'd expected Esah to say faced with June after three years, it hadn't been this.

June stared and stared and couldn't seem to help what she said next either. "The math wouldn't add up, Mak."

Again, for the third time, Esah said, "June," and like June's voice had released a dam she started crying, really softly, the only sound a sort of gasping for air. June had not blinked once but now she said softly, "Oh," and went straight into her mother's arms.

It was muffled, but Aisha could hear, "I'm sorry," and she wasn't sure if that was Esah or June. She heard a muffled, gaspy, "Sorry, I'm sorry," in reply, and she supposed it didn't matter, then.

Aisha had not seen her mother cry for as long as she could remember. She supposed she *could* remember, but the memories flickered. She felt hollow and empty watching it. She couldn't figure out why. She felt like maybe she should be joining in the hug, although the very thought made her want to step away.

June and Esah gasped for breath and held onto each other for dear life, while the wind whistled through the leaves of the heavy trees and Walter felt for Aisha's hand and held it.

She remembered, half a moment later, to close her fingers around his, even though they felt slightly numb.

The small someone hid behind June's legs still and said, "Who *are* these people?"

The Truth

(an interval)

The pure and simple truth was that Aisha was furious at June.

She had not realised this until she saw Esah and June embracing, but now from blankness it rose white-hot in her, the way it sometimes did when she and Walter fought and she had to work so hard to tamp it down. It was a sharp terrible jagged sort of anger, and she was surprised at it.

The story, of course, was this:

Uncle Amin had died, and Nek Kah had taken a fall, and Nek Dan could not be without the someone he'd loved for fifty years. And then Pak had died, long and drawn-out until you could see the bones through his skin. And then Esah could not live with this – and how could you blame her? Aisha couldn't, Aisha couldn't – so they had moved across the country and for a long time their mother had merely existed, a firmly substantial sort of ghost who scolded at June to come back right after school, no dawdling, and firmly disallowed any waves past their waists.

That had been that. You could not talk to a ghost who would fade at the sound of memories. So it had for so long been Aisha and June, the tale-teller and her eager recipient, the bed across the room. Esah stared into space, or the window, or her hands, nothing but her body in the room. June noticed – and she noticed Aisha noticing. Then June's voice rose, either sharp or teasing or distracting, across the room, making sure Aisha's thoughts were on other things. And when Esah was a strict kind of ghost, fading into the kitchen chair or under her blanket, June's voice would meander along the room, one night drawing stories of their grandparents and their father, the next, far-off lands where she and Aisha would travel to one day.

Then June had gone and her voice with her, and it had been so hard to remember the tales she had told so it was easier to stop trying. June had always been the one who properly *remembered* them, remembered them so vividly. Without her, many memories became just stories Aisha had been told, and without her she had no one to corroborate any memories.

Aisha stood at the open door, such a bright green, and she fought to keep this anger at June down. The new skin itched and itched and broke open. She closed her eyes and thought of how much harder than bravery this was.

Fleabag rubbed himself against her ankles, velvety, and Aisha opened her eyes and saw she was still standing.

Where June Was

(the present)

June, wiping tears off her cheeks, took Aisha by the shoulders and said, "Sha." She hugged Aisha, close and firm, and Aisha, after a moment of furiously not wanting to, hugged her back. There was nothing else she could do, and everyone was watching. June smelled like she always had: faintly of vanilla, faintly of freshly-cut roses, the soap she'd stockpiled way before the Announcement.

June took a step back and said to Walter and his parents steadily, if her breathing was still hitching, "Hi, I'm June, the prodigal daughter." She managed a little wave, like it was amusing.

Walter said, "I'm Walter," after a moment, and they shook hands.

"We're Walter's parents," said Elizabeth, and they all shook hands too.

Beneath the anger that still threatened to rise in her throat and exit her, it all felt slightly surreal. Aisha had met Walter a few months after June had left. She had never seriously considered them meeting, too busy trying to strip June from her thoughts like she'd stripped her sheets. It was like cleaning a new wound. You wouldn't think the plaster would have cause to meet the sharp object.

"Oh, wow," June said, noticing the campervan and blinking.

"It's a funny design, isn't it?" Robert asked affably, gesturing at the florid green, the tentacles, and the eyes.

"Interesting design," June said faintly.

Aisha wasn't looking at her, but she could feel June look at her a bit, like she was trying to catch her eye about the campervan. Aisha refused to look back.

"Got it off a friend!" Robert said. "He's got bits and bobs like this all over his place. This is a lovely house."

"It was my grandparents'," June said.

"Yes, your mother mentioned," Elizabeth said pleasantly.

They exchanged a few more pleasantries about the structure of the house and the large compound. Fleabag made his way through their legs and peered past the front door.

"Is the cat yours?" June asked. Aisha could feel her sister's eyes on her again, like she wanted her to answer. When Aisha didn't, June said, "Interesting colour."

Fleabag made an indignant meow at her like he had heard the intonation of *interesting*, stretching the *ow* out to demonstrate his hurt feelings.

"That's Fleabag," Aisha said, trying not to sound curt and feeling irrationally defensive of the ridiculous cat. "He's ours. I guess."

Fleabag blinked, deliberate and approving, at her. Then

they all took off their shoes, stepped inside properly, and he slunk in, like it was just another house that was his now.

The house inside was all rich brown wood, airy, clean. There was Islamic calligraphy on one wall, ruby red carpet on the floor, and pictures of June and Aisha, young and grinning, on all the surfaces. Faced with all of it like this, Aisha remembered more and more: Nek Dan and his newspaper in the heavy wooden rocking chair, Nek Kah humming happily over the *dhal* she was making. *Sinetrons* in the daytime and Raj Kapoor films on at night. The house had never been quiet, something always murmuring in company.

She felt, unreasonably, even more furious at June. How much had Aisha forgotten because June had just up and left?

Esah was bending down and saying to the little someone, "My name is Auntie Esah," and Aisha shook her head slightly to clear it and bent down too.

"I'm Aisha," she said.

Small Someone had straight black hair that flopped into almond eyes and was wearing blue Big Bird pyjamas. He looked at her very seriously. "How do you know June?" he asked, in a piping little voice.

"Well . . ." Esah hesitated and looked up at June, who nodded. "I'm her mother."

Small Someone's eyes grew wide. "I didn't know June had a mother."

"Oh," Esah said, and closed her mouth, and didn't say anything else.

June looked quickly at her mother. "I did too tell you about my mum," she said sternly to the child. "I said she lived very far away."

"Well I forgot," Small Someone said simply.

"She has a sister, too," Aisha said. "Me." Had June not told him *that*? Of course June hadn't told him. Aisha told herself not to care. What would you expect from someone who had walked away and not come back even once?

"What's your name?" Esah asked him.

"I'm James Yeo Zhi Wei," Small Someone said with great gravitas. He stuck out his hand and shook both of theirs. "It's nice to meet you." He ruined his grave countenance summarily by grinning up at June for approval.

"Excellent manners, little man," June said, taking him by the hand. "Let's come along to the kitchen, shall we? Lunch is almost ready."

She looked apologetically at her guests. "I didn't prepare enough for anyone else, I think, let me check . . ."

"That's fine, there's packed food," said Elizabeth. She and Robert went out to get it.

Esah followed June and James to the kitchen. Just like that, the first moments were over. Aisha had met her sister and nothing earth-shattering had happened. Just this quietly jagged fury inside.

She didn't immediately move. Slowly she rested her head against Walter's chest, and his arms came up to wrap around her. He had been hovering around her ever since the front door, a hand on her elbow or a shoulder against hers every so often.

"I'm angry at her," she said, muffled. It was easier to say into his shirt, which smelled of clean, fresh detergent. That didn't seem to quite cover everything she felt, but she was testing it out on her tongue.

Over the top of her head, he reassured her, "That's all right."

That terrible annoyance flared back up. She said snappishly, drawing back a bit, "It's *not*. Don't make it sound like it is."

Walter sighed and dropped his arms and said, "But it really is. Being angry is absolutely fine."

"Why are *you* never angry?" she demanded.

He narrowed his eyes slightly. "I do get angry," he said, and didn't elaborate further.

She let go and after a moment, he did too. Then she was angrier at herself. She didn't know why she had said that, why she had asked that. She touched his cheek and couldn't say anything more. Walter smiled at her, lifting the corner of his mouth sort of sadly.

"I'm sorry," Aisha said.

"I know," Walter said. "It's fine."

It didn't really sound like it was fine, but he was already turning away.

In the kitchen, June was ladling some soup into a bowl for James, who was washing his hands carefully.

The kitchen looked much the same as Aisha was starting to remember. Walls tinted burnt-orange, large wood stove in the back, heavy dining table with ten elaborately carved chairs. Nek Dan had painstakingly carved all of them, bent close to the heavy wood with his chisel. Esah was sitting on one. Aisha wondered what it meant that she now had come back to the house she'd covered in plastic and packed into boxes and left for good within days of her parents' death. That she was facing all these things she'd tried to bury so they didn't overwhelm her all at once, and she was now facing them all at once.

Her mother looked fine, focused on James. It was infuriating how she could be so calm, so interested in James, so easily asking questions of June, when it was Aisha who was fighting to tamp down the feelings, the fury.

"Then his mother passed away," June was saying. "But before that she asked me to make sure he was taken care of."

"So you thought the best way to do this was to take him in yourself," Esah said, and Aisha wondered if she was thinking about Arif, who had taken in a grand total of five stray cats and seven stray dogs, one hurt squirrel, and several people without shelter at night, in the years they'd had together.

"Well . . . yes," June said. "I was also—" She cleared her throat, but soldiered on. "I was also lonely."

There was a studied, uncomfortable silence, broken by Elizabeth and Robert coming in with the leftover curry.

They heated it up in the large stone pot over the stove Nek Kah had bent over for years. Like a flickering image, Aisha could almost see her.

Walter also cleared his throat. "I don't think we've met, James," he said, pulling out a chair and sitting down opposite James, who had started scooping the soup up into his mouth. "I'm Walter."

"Okay," said James, sticking out his hand across the table and nearly upending his soup. Walter took the damp-looking little hand gamely. "Are you June's brother?"

"No, no," said Walter hastily. "I'm Aisha's friend."

"Do you like Big Bird?" James asked suspiciously.

"I like Elmo better myself," Walter said. "Sometimes the Cookie Monster is my favourite though. Sometimes Oscar."

James made a considering sound at this. "That's a lot," he said.

"I like all of them," Walter said easily.

"Elmo's a bit stupid," James decided. "He doesn't know anything."

"James, that's not very nice," June said without turning around.

Fleabag slunk orangely into the room at the smell of food and James's eyes grew wide again, evidently noticing him for the first time.

"Kitty!" he said enthusiastically.

"Don't give him your food," June said. "James! He'll get his own." But James had almost flung his spoon across the room in his excitement to feed Fleabag, so June started cleaning up the soup that had splattered about.

Their mother watched her do this, her expression something complicated and loving.

They drew up chairs and sat around the table to begin eating. Elizabeth asked in a transparent attempt to break the rather awkward silence, "Do you grow any fruits?"

She'd been eyeing the mangoes and rambutans, Aisha surmised.

"There's a vegetable patch, and then in the front there's the trees," said June. "They're pretty easy. They look after themselves. And then we get cucumbers and beans from the neighbours out in front."

They lapsed into a slightly stilted, newly-acquainted conversation about crops, turning into a slightly stilted, newly-acquainted conversation about how the community worked in the neighbourhood. There was a seventy-six-year-old doctor whose wife had passed away and who had no one else, who was looking after the medical needs of the neighbourhood. There was a field a little ways away, with a few cows, and when one was eaten everybody got beef for a week. Robert was especially interested in the Second-World-War-era generator Aisha's grand-father had apparently bought, and was invited to look at it after the meal. The conversation limped steadily along. Aisha averted her eyes from June and was able to swallow mouthfuls of curry down.

"What do you do?" Esah asked eventually. "I mean, what have you been doing these days?"

"James is more than enough to keep me busy," June

said, slanting a look at the child in question, who was attempting to surreptitiously feed Fleabag under the table.

"No," James said. "You've been outside digging!"

"Yes," June conceded. To the table at large, she said, "Mostly I've been busy digging the bunker."

A Conversation with Arif

(ten years ago)

Aisha's father had smelled different, smelled like medicine and sometimes slightly like vomit. But when she came into his arms he held her just as strongly, even if her mother did now tend to come in to say things like *Be careful* and *Let him rest.*

Aisha, back from school and finished with her lunch, was about to run sweatily into his room when she heard voices coming from it. June had gone up earlier, but Aisha had thought she'd gone to their room. June, newly twelve, was beginning to be fussy about her own space, carving blocks of time away from Aisha when she would have otherwise dragged her around to play their childhood games.

"It's not fair," June was saying. "I want to—"

"Then do it," their father was saying, as tired as he always sounded these days, voice wearing thin.

"It would be three days," June said, in a resigned sort of way. "Mak wouldn't go for it. And we need to be here, for you—"

"I'll talk to her," Arif interrupted, in a voice that brooked no argument. "June . . ."

There was silence for a while, silence that stretched on long enough that Aisha peeked around the door.

June was sitting on the edge of the bed. Arif was propped up on three pillows, gaunter than ever, hair flat from where he had been lying in bed all morning. On the bedside table next to him was his favourite *ayam masak lemak*, left untouched; he had no appetite for anything these days. He was utterly focused on his daughter.

"You can do anything you want to do, June," he said

very seriously, reaching up and catching her chin between his thumb and forefinger. "Don't you know that? You can do anything you could ever want."

Bunker

(the present)

There was a silence, broken by James scooping up the last of his soup loudly.

"*Sayang*, it's just that the scientists—" Esah said, and June's head whipped towards her – it had probably been the unconscious, new-old use of the pet name. "They said it'd be no use."

"They said *most* would be no use," June corrected. "If it's deep enough we have a chance. That's still a chance. And I'm planning to make mine really deep."

"It's going to be the deepest bunker EVER," James chirped up happily. "And I'm helping!"

Aisha looked at Walter, who was studying his curry, reaching up to rub his neck, and she looked at Esah, who was studying June with worry. Robert and Elizabeth were exchanging looks.

Fleabag gnawed on his chicken bone.

"How deep is it?"

"Deep enough," June said. "It's thirty feet so far."

"That's quite impressive work," Robert commented. "Especially if you don't have the proper tools."

"I've got a few shovels," June said. "And well, you know, a small excavator. I've been trying to figure that bit of machinery out mostly."

"I've helped," James declared. "June makes me bring drinks for her over and over again and she says if she doesn't have refreshmerents the hole's not getting dug."

June grinned at James. "And you've been a big help."

Robert made a humming noise, and looked at Elizabeth again, this time considering. Elizabeth looked back, raising her eyebrows, and it was again like they were having a conversation in a language no one else was privy to.

"Where did you get an excavator?" Walter asked.

"I found it here. I guess we've always had one," June said.

"Nek Dan was going to dig their own swimming pool," Esah said in a faraway voice. "Before Nek Kah's fall." Aisha watched her, and so did June, watched as she seemed to dip into that space where neither of them could reach her.

But their mother looked back at June. "We'll help." Her voice was suddenly resolute.

"Really?" June said, looking up at her mother.

"We'll help," said Esah again.

June seemed cracked-open with hope. Staring at her mother like that, her eyes were so bright. Esah nodded, her face spreading with what looked like longing, but manifested itself into a smile.

The moment held and held. Across the table, Elizabeth and Richard were nodding, and Aisha could see it, the first sparks of cautious hope in the way they looked at each other. Even Walter was looking at June, silent but listening.

Aisha couldn't help it. The rage pushed the words out into her mouth and onto her tongue.

She said, "It's impractical. It's a waste of our time."

The faces all turned to look at her. She did not want to read what she saw in them.

"It's worth a shot," June began, but Aisha cut in, "We can't just waste time entertaining your false hope especially when we've got so little time left."

Someone inhaled. Probably Esah, possibly Walter. Aisha didn't stop. It felt like another argument with Walter, except this time she wasn't going to feel bad.

"Thirty feet is nothing, it's got to be at least, what, hundreds, and that's— It's not only impractical, it's unfair to us that just because you want something, all of us are sacrificing our time—"

"I never asked any of you to sacrifice your time," June said, eyes narrowing, hands defensively up.

Aisha opened her mouth, thinking about what exactly June knew about sacrifice, but Walter said quietly into the silence, "It's not impossible."

Aisha said, "It really is, so don't flatter her, you don't know anything about what she's like. The world doesn't revolve around *you*," she snapped at June, turning back to her, "and what you want, at the expense of other people who want to help. At the expense of their time and their kindness and their— you don't own them: the world isn't yours."

She rather thought she would have to scrape back her chair and storm off, but – she'd been in the middle of lunch, and the politeness she'd been raised with restrained her from leaving her plate like that. Then silence prevailed, and she felt growing embarrassment, warm in her neck, her cheeks. She did not feel bad for shouting at June, but she had done it in front of everyone. She stared fixedly at the food, but she could feel June and Walter's eyes on her. She did not know if their expressions were accusing.

Robert and Elizabeth had busied themselves with their food as well. Aisha didn't know where Esah was looking.

James, at last, said, "I don't *like* her, June. She's mean to you."

June didn't answer. Aisha felt unreasonably like screaming at this, or sobbing. She scooped the last spoonful up and swallowed it, pushing down the petty *Well she was mean to me*. It tasted like nothing, and she picked the plate up and washed it at the sink.

She walked out very steadily. Out of the kitchen, then out of the house, into the grass. She walked until she reached the back.

Nek Kah flickered in and out of memory, bending over the pots, and Nek Dan hacked away at branches with an axe. She could see neither of their faces.

The garden was wild and lovely and overgrown. Another heavy rambutan tree curved branches over one corner.

A large square-approximate hole lay dug in the middle of it all, where the brook had been. It took up about half the backyard. Aisha bypassed it, bypassed the small yellow excavator beside it, and went to the back, where the rambutan tree stood. She stopped next to it and stared up at the sky, filtered by the leaves. Fleabag mewed at her feet quite suddenly. Aisha almost jumped.

"I bet you think it's a good idea too," she said bitterly, but without much heat behind it.

Fleabag just mewed again plaintively. He did not care that she had shouted; he merely wanted to be petted, and he wanted to be petted now.

"You ask for so much for such a tiny little . . . thing," she said. "And I really wish you would leave me alone." But she sank down anyway and gathered him close, pressing his warm, breathing body against her cheek.

Under the Rambutan Tree
(the present)

Aisha sat down under the tree. She was so tired, unreasonably lethargic, pressure in her temples like the beginnings of a headache. But the rambutan tree offered cool shade, a breeze caressing her skin every once in a while.

She sat for a long time, so long that the afternoon lessened its heavy hot pressure and began to grow golden instead. She almost dozed off, leaning against its trunk, the rough solid bark, but she blinked and heard the sound of footsteps on grass instead. Beside her Fleabag breathed evenly in and out, his small body moving with it. He was already sleeping, ear twitching contently once or twice like he was dreaming of good things.

She heard James's chirping voice next. "And this is where I fell and scraped my knee on the stone. June cleaned it up real well and I was so brave even though there was blood."

"That's really good of you," Robert said, and there they were looking down into the hole. Robert was holding James's hand. He looked solid and comfortable like this, keeping James from wriggling further forward in a very practised manner. Aisha didn't feel bad for shouting at June, but she felt more embarrassed now, even slightly guilty, that she had said it was impossible in front of Robert. Robert, who had his wife, who had a son who had had the world ahead of him. He had not deserved to hear saving them was impossible.

James said, "We took ages to do this and June says I mustn't even go near it as I might fall." June had put in place flimsy precautions against this: wire netting over

174

the hole, held in place by sticks dug in the earth. "I'm not allowed to go back here without suverpision."

"I think it's supervision," Robert advised kindly. He was looking down into the hole, squatting over its edge and inspecting it carefully. Aisha remembered he'd been an engineer for twenty years. He looked up and noticed the large metal sheets propped against the wire fence, and then he noticed Aisha.

He murmured something to James, who squinted at Aisha suspiciously, little face scrunching up, but he followed Robert towards her.

"Napping?" he asked. "It's a good day for it."

Aisha tried to smile and it felt rusty. "Almost," she said. Then she remembered her manners and said, "I'm sorry about the scene at lunch."

Robert shook his head. "Family, you know?" he said, dismissing the heavy implications of this word with a wave of his big hand. "Though I think your sister would like to talk to you."

"More like yell at me," Aisha murmured. She looked towards the house. "I'll go in."

"No, we'll get her," Robert said. "I think you need the space out here." He looked around, taking it all in: the wide sky, the heavy branches of the tree, the years the garden held. "It's good space. Good earth," he said, nodding. "Good space."

"I'll go inside," Aisha said, "you don't have to go in, it *is* good space, and you should enjoy it like you were going to."

"Family," he said and waved a hand again, like it could dismiss her protests and explain everything away all at once. Aisha guessed it did. He smiled at her, so much Walter in his eyes, the gently enquiring arch of his thick eyebrows, and started walking away.

Aisha did not know what to do with Walter's parents' kindnesses.

James went with him, but after a few steps ran back to Aisha. He said, "Be nice to June!"

She wasn't nice to me, Aisha immediately wanted to snap. "I'll try my best, James," she promised instead. She watched them go, and then let her head thud softly back onto the trunk. The branches and leaves let some more golden light filter through. It was getting on in the day.

When she heard the door open again she readied herself for June's presence, but as she was trying to keep her gaze low and her feelings under control she realised it was Elizabeth's sensible brown shoes coming into view.

Elizabeth didn't sit next to Aisha, but she shielded her eyes from the sun with a slender hand and held out a glass of something pink with the other. "Guava juice," she said. The glass was sweating with condensation.

Aisha apologised again. "I'm sorry about lunch, I know I was out of—"

"These things are complicated," Elizabeth said, demonstrating a wave that looked like a slightly more graceful version of Robert's, then another wave when Aisha tried to get up to join her. "Don't apologise. Sit and drink. It's a warm day, you don't want to overheat."

Aisha complied. The liquid was cool and thick, making its slow, sweet way down her throat. "It's good, Auntie," she said. "You always make it so well."

"Years of practice," Elizabeth said. "You need to get the consistency right, you know? You don't want it to be so sugary, either."

"It's perfect," Aisha said.

Elizabeth smiled, then seemed to regard Aisha with some measure of thoughtfulness. "When Walter was younger, maybe two or three, he got sick and wouldn't drink water. He wouldn't drink milk or tea or anything. I was getting worried." She frowned slightly at the memory. "It was the only thing he would drink. Juice."

"He never told me that."

"He probably doesn't remember." Elizabeth made a sound that was too genteel to be a snort, but was decidedly less polite than a sniff. "I was sleep deprived with worry, squeezing oranges out into the blender, getting seeds everywhere. The things you do for your children."

"I'm sure he's grateful for everything you do." Aisha meant it. Walter had had a happy childhood; he spoke of it with the same offhanded fondness people spoke of something they took for granted and didn't think much about. He loved his parents and spoke of them in much the same way: amused, understated, a steady and universal truth of his world. *They're great, for parents.*

"You don't become a parent for gratitude." Elizabeth sounded wry, but she tucked a stray lock of hair behind one ear and looked up at the leaves, the sunlight that drifted dreamily through them. She squinted, her gaze caught on something different.

"Big rambutans," she said. "Healthy, too. You can see the colour, they're almost ripe. *Bidang tanah ke manah.* Aisha," she said, addressing her directly, looking at her with that same thoughtfulness, "you're a good kid. Your mother knows that. And your sister too."

Aisha didn't know how to respond to this. It was a simple sentiment, and it wasn't like it was something unfamiliar. She knew she had been a good child, or at least she had tried, had tried to get good grades and come home early, had tried not to be difficult for her mother. Hearing it like this, though, put so plainly, it seemed like more than it was.

"I could try harder," she said.

"Yes, couldn't we all?" agreed Elizabeth. "You're still a good kid. Come, give me the glass." Having retrieved it, she smiled at Aisha, the flash of her smile familiar from Walter's thousands, and walked away. She had dropped this kindness into Aisha's lap as easily and offhandedly as her son did most things.

Aisha felt a little better.

An Apology

(the present)

It didn't last for long. When June came out, Aisha again felt wild white-hot anger rise in her, watching her sister out of the corner of her eye. June carefully crossed the backyard, eyes on her face the entire time, and sat down cross-legged opposite her.

She had grown her hair out, and there was a new scar on her forearm. She could have gotten it mountaineering or making dinner, who knew? Not her mother or her sister, who she'd left behind while she'd gone anywhere she wanted. Her eyes were somehow older, like she had gotten what she wanted; like she'd seen the world and eaten it all up.

"I know you're still very angry with me," June was saying abruptly. "And I know you have every right to be."

Aisha said nothing.

"Tell me how much you're angry with me, it'll help," June said, like she knew anything about what would help. "It'll really help – just say it all, say everything you need to say."

Aisha stared fixedly at the hole over her left shoulder instead.

June sighed and pushed a lock of pink hair over one sticky-out ear. The words came slowly out of her. "I left, I know I left. When you obviously needed my support the most, I left."

Aisha had nothing to say to that, really. June was stating the obvious.

"Come on, Aisha," June said after they had sat a bit and Aisha had stayed motionless. Her voice contained the slightest edge of exasperation.

Aisha was suddenly reminded of countless arguments

from her early teenage years she hadn't thought of in a long time, shouting the worst things they could think of across their shared room. It inspired a very childish feeling in her. She stayed silent.

"You can't not talk to me for ever," June told her.

She seemed to forget that Aisha had thought she was never even going to see her again, up until today. That up until a few hours ago she hadn't even known if June was alive.

"Aisha, look at me," June said. There was an edge to her voice that could have been annoyance or panic. "You can't."

Can't I? Aisha thought, not without some satisfaction.

"All right," said June, running short fingers through her hair and changing tactics. "You're old enough. You have to understand I *had* to." Aisha raised her eyebrows at the middle distance. "You know what it was like. I couldn't do anything. I told you I couldn't stay in that house. I shouldn't have left you but I needed to—"

Aisha said loudly, because this was just *ridiculous*, "I needed you!"

June shut up.

"I needed you to not disappear," Aisha gritted out, and then ground her teeth together again, still not looking at her sister.

"I didn't know how much," June said gently. Then hesitantly, in the silence, she said, "But you must see how I had to go. I *am* sorry I didn't get in touch, I just didn't know how to do it—"

This made Aisha's anger spill over into her voice, syllables coming out cutting. "I don't care."

"Well," said June after a moment, sounding choked, which just made Aisha angrier.

"You don't just get to say *sorry*." She sneered the word. The cutting meanness of her own voice surprised her.

"I'm not *just* saying sorry, I'm trying to explain!" June said, so Aisha said snidely, "Well it's too late for that now, isn't it?"

"I need you to listen," June said, almost sounding stern now, older-sisterly, something Aisha hadn't heard in years and which made her incredulous with fury at the thought that June felt she had the right any more.

"When you left it was so hard to remember – and you know Mak never talks about it – *I* needed to remember Nek Kah and Nek Dan and Pak. *I* needed you to at least call, once in a while, and you never did. *I* needed your help and I needed you not to leave, *more* than you needed to go, and you know what? I hate you for it."

This was her sister. Aisha hurled the words over the space between them.

"I hate you for going to find yourself or whatever and leaving me behind, and now I'll never get my turn. I hate you for going off and not knowing that I wanted to do medicine in Edinburgh and work in KL, and I hate you for getting three years full of what you wanted while Mak pretended nothing was wrong. I hate you because I hate her, but how can I hate her when she was trying so hard not to fall apart? But you – it was supposed to be *us*."

The breeze gently blew and the leaves rustled. Aisha looked up, up, at the branches and the golden light filtering through and tried her best. Leaves, the light, the tide, coming in and going out and coming in again.

June said, "It *is* us."

"It quite obviously isn't!" Aisha felt she had made herself clear and she didn't feel any better about it.

June said, very low, like she was whispering, "I'm sorry."

Aisha looked at June, who repeated it. "I am. I'm sorry. I didn't think about you much, did I?"

"No." Aisha wished she would stop. She really hated how she could just say *I'm sorry* like it was some sort of balm over a wound, like the past three years had never happened. Like her skin didn't itch itch *itch*.

She hated how she would probably end up forgiving her anyway, in the end. How could you *not*, so close to the end? That was the problem here: no more life to live. No more grudges to be held. Even when you wanted so badly to hold on to them.

June's brow was furrowed. Her eyes were distressed and contrite, glassy with the tears she wasn't shedding yet. Aisha fiercely tried to ignore this and couldn't. She was still angry, but this was still her big sister.

"I still know I had to go." June's gaze sought out Aisha's, like she needed absolution for saying this, but she was saying it anyway. "I'm not sorry for leaving. But for what it did to you – I feel like *shit*," June said. "For not calling. Not coming back. Just because I was scared of what you and Mak would say. That was the reason. I was scared."

"That's no reason," Aisha said.

"That's the only reason I've got. That's what I'm sorry for. For that – for that I don't know what to do. How to fix us. Or even if I can."

"Maybe you can't," Aisha said, and looked away when June's face crumpled fully, when she started crying.

There was a long while in which no one said anything

but June sobbed, loud and sharp and almost despairing, like she was mourning something.

Like she was mourning her sister. Aisha didn't look back at her. She didn't. June cried and cried and tried to compose herself, gasping with it. Aisha thought of her saying *I'm not sorry for leaving*. She thought of her saying *I was scared*.

She did say, "I brought you your pink sheets," because angry as she was, she was still there. June had no business mourning someone who was still there.

This cracked June open a little bit, and she sniffed and wiped the back of her hand over her nose. "Aisha, I'm *sorry* I didn't come back. I'm going to do *whatever* I can . . ."

Looking at her like this, snot running down her nose, Aisha's anger died down a little. It wasn't as white-hot, at least. This was still her big sister and she wasn't supposed to look like that, wasn't supposed to sound heartbroken.

"Well," she said, trying to keep any kind of emotion out of her voice. "I guess you needed to. Or whatever. Do the Kerouac thing."

"And you needed me," June said, and Aisha could not dispute this. "I thought you'd be fine – Mak was much more lenient with you, and she'd gotten much better, and I figured it was only a couple of years more and you'd survived that long. I didn't call because the months passed and I thought you were angry at me for leaving like I did and I *couldn't*. I didn't think about you and what you needed as much. And I'm sorry."

"I don't really hate you," Aisha said, after a while.

"I love you," June said, now openly crying. Aisha inched forward until she could put her arm about her shoulders, touch her pink head. June had always been *better* at crying: angry or distressed or grieving, her tears ran as freely as anything. Aisha's throat was tight and the boiling resentment she felt towards June had died down very quickly, if not dissipated, but she could not cry.

"Tell me what you did," she said, quietly, as the sun tiredly faded out. "Tell me everything."

June told her about working and saving up to add to

the money their grandparents had left her, about Iran and Bolivia, about Argentina and South Korea, about Rome and Luxembourg. Aisha could not speak – these were all, now, places unreachable. Again June was spinning stories in the space between them and again they were so, so unreachable to Aisha. Stories about grandparents she'd barely known and a father whose scent was slowly slipping away. Now they were stories about large, beautiful ruins and sparkling oceans and sun-baked cities and the chill of mountains she'd never see up close. Always death stealing these memories for Aisha, the history of the stories and the promise of future ones. Always June crossing the finish line while Aisha had barely started running.

June told her about coming back and the journey to Melaka, to meeting James and his dying mother along the way.

"I missed you so much," June said.

You had a whole life, Aisha wanted to say. She felt robbed and hurt and split-open. The wound broke open and healed and did it over and over again. But June's words wound themselves into the deepening dusk as softly padded as Fleabag's paws, picturing her life for Aisha and reconstructing her memories with it. The white-hot anger was gone for the moment. Aisha was just listening, as she always did.

A Story about Walter

(two years and eight months ago)

The boy in her class who had on a T-shirt with a bulldog on it opened his full mouth and said, "See the thing about that is you assume Cleopatra's affection for Antony," and started on a speech why said affection could be disproven.

Aisha leaned back in her chair and uncapped her pen, wondering if she should be writing this down. She would ask someone, but there was no one to ask. She'd been at this programme a week and hadn't made an effort to make friends.

It wasn't that she hadn't wanted to. It was just so much *effort*. All her energy was expended on trying to patch up the wound that gaped open in her room. New skin hadn't started knitting over, even if it had already been three months.

But the boy sat back and Aisha opened her mouth almost inadvertently. "Cleopatra can't show weakness, she rules a nation and as an unmarried woman she has to be extra careful with how she's perceived," she said. "It doesn't mean she doesn't care."

The boy who would soon come to be known as Walter turned in his seat to look. Aisha took in his brown eyes, his soft-looking hair, the crookedness of his canines as he smiled delightedly at her.

Later on, he caught up to her and said, "Interesting opinion. Not that I agreed with it, but—"

"You have something against women in power?" Aisha said. Strangely enough it came out teasing.

"Just Cleopatra," Walter said, falling into step.

His voice was a warm-sounding sort of voice. It reminded her of Sunday morning in the kitchen with the smell of baking, or fresh laundry. It wasn't a lot of effort. It was no effort at all.

Walter loved a lot of things, because he was never going to decide on one and he was always hungry to find more. He loved coral documentaries and DC movies and trashy reality television. He loved cats and squirrels and stick insects. He loved the dreaminess of holidays with his family and the complexities of algebra and the world-building of fantasy novels.

Walter was so many things, because he was never going to decide on one. He was short-sighted and pretended he wasn't, and he was impatient with people who pretended they knew more than they did. He was spoiled and sweet, snappish and steady, as stubborn as she was and far, far more fidgety. Walter was funny in a way that made you feel funny too, and he was empathetic in a way that made you feel like you were listened to. Aisha didn't know all of this that first day, but she would grow to love it all fiercely.

They texted back and forth until one night he'd called

her up, and then they'd talked until dawn, something inside her unfurling into a sweet yearning. He took her paintballing and to modern art galleries, and they cursed each other out as their shots missed the targets, tried to make intelligent observations about confusing installations. She took him kayaking and food-hunting, and they nearly upended their kayak against jagged rocks, bought dodgy-looking meats from food vans that turned out delicious. They went to the beach and held hands by the water. She watched him – all the clean lines of him, all his careless movements – and wanted things she couldn't name, a lovely ache that warmed her inside and out.

Aisha thought of quiet gentle things when she thought of him. She thought of golden sunlight in the evening and the warmth of her mother's smile. She thought of freshly-washed sheets and the velvet of a cat's fur. There was something inside him that was endlessly gentle and unceasingly restless, all at once, the steady promise and beginning of so many different things. It held.

Falling for him wasn't some sudden shocking thing. There was no suddenness about it, no tide coming in she hadn't realised. It wasn't dramatic and it didn't involve anything as scary and violent as falling. It rose and rose in her until she could not bear it sometimes, that feeling of pure helium happiness. She told him about June and tested the wound gingerly and found that the new skin held, perhaps because of the balm of his steady gaze. She brought him home and watched Esah quietly appraise him; watched him squint over her recipe books in pure appreciation and help with dinner; watched her learn to love him too.

Perhaps one of the things Aisha loved most about him, in the end, was that he was there. He was quiet but he was never absent. He debated books with her and sang along off-key to songs on the radio and shot paintballs like it was war. He argued with her and loved her as fiercely as anything, you could see it right there in his unwavering gaze.

She came home that first night and wished she could tell June about him.

Aisha Finds a Book

(the present)

It turned out that while she had been outside, Elizabeth and Walter and Esah had been getting the rooms ready. Mothballed sheets came out of closets – "We'll wash them in a bit, but this'll do," – and onto mattresses. One room for Elizabeth and Robert, one for Walter, one for Esah, one for Aisha. June and James shared a room down the hall, James beside June's mattress in a car-shaped bed.

Esah watched them anxiously as they came in, and Aisha smiled tiredly at her.

It was how she felt – tired. Like after all that anger the well was coming up empty. Dinner was a quiet affair, with

197

Elizabeth and Robert retiring early. June took James up to bed after his head drooped sleepily onto her shoulder in the kitchen.

In the living room there was a creamy, soft sofa, with throws draped around the back. Aisha curled up on it and opened one of Nek Kah's Malay novels, filled with affairs and tears. There was an inscription on the first page:

Anika,

Selamat hari jadi, sayang.

Hati saya hanya milik awak, selama-lamanya.

Danial

Aisha traced her finger slowly over the words. *Happy birthday, my love. My heart is yours, forever.*

The lamp was dimming low when Walter sank into the sofa next to her. Aisha didn't turn to look at him, but she lowered her head to his shoulder. He smelled vaguely of clean sweat and still, faintly, of cologne.

He pressed his nose into the top of her head. "Are you upset with me?" he asked.

Aisha said, "I'm never upset with you." This was true. Anger rose up in her and directed itself, impossibly, towards one of the few people she loved so deeply, but it was never *at* him. After she had stopped being angry she never knew why she had been angry in the first place.

"Hm," Walter said in that way he had where he didn't really believe what was coming out of your mouth. "Sounded very much like you were."

"I'm angry at everything," Aisha said, surprised at this truth once it had left her mouth. "I think I'm projecting."

"Angry at your sister?"

"I was," Aisha agreed. "But I might not be any more. I don't know. Maybe I still am, and there just isn't time any more to be."

"That's still anger," Walter offered.

"But I think it might be more than that." A lot more. So much. Like Aisha's old depths were plumbing new ones. "I didn't realise how much it was until I said all those things to June."

She told him about it, how it felt, sitting under the tree and her voice rising in something that felt an awful lot like relief, then June's tears, drenching her shoulder and cleansing old wounds.

He listened like he always did, attentive and quiet, and then he said, "So not just your sister. You're angry at everything," very succinctly.

"I haven't figured it out," Aisha admitted. "I'm just starting to."

"So you know it's not me," Walter asked-said.

"I know it's not you." Here Aisha twisted from his shoulder and looked at him closely, their noses inches away. "I'm sorry about that."

"You should be," Walter said seriously, eyes clear. "You've been snappish for months." He sighed. "It's not that I don't understand, Sha, but for as long as we can, I want to be *happy* with you."

"I don't know how to express things properly, I think," Aisha said. "I'm so sorry. I—*Walter.*" He had looked away, and she moved to chase his gaze. She was so tired and it was easier to be honest now. "I was planning to be with you for a long time, and that's why I'm so angry around you."

"Do you think we would have stayed together?" Walter asked. "If this wasn't happening?"

Aisha thought about their future, arrayed in front of her, the progression of their decades. They would have gotten engaged some years after university, saving up for a place to stay. Fleabag moving into their first apartment with them and yowling at their cocker spaniel or their turtle or their guinea pig. Movie nights at the local theatre and Walter coming up to her after a day in the hospital, holding a squirming child.

They would have named their first one Amin but Uncle Amin was dead now, and she could not remember her grandparents. She could barely even remember her father. There would be no one left to remember them. Oh, oh, she was so *tired*.

Walter brushed his hand across her cheek, very tenderly, when she didn't answer. "Goodnight, Sha," he said, expression shadowed, lashes fragile against the curve of his cheek.

The sensation of his touch lingered on her skin. Aisha almost said *Don't go,* but in the end she didn't say anything at all. Walter went upstairs, his footsteps soft, and he didn't come back down.

James
(the present)

Aisha overslept again, the longest she'd ever overslept. Hot rays of afternoon light poured into her room, a particularly floral one with a heavy dark wardrobe and headboard. She was sweating and humid: she pushed heavy locks of hair off her neck, feeling immediate relief.

The clock said two fifteen and she rose sharply, wondering how anybody had let her sleep until this hour.

The wooden door creaked open. Aisha went to wash up, pouring water over her face and tying her hair back. She felt slightly better, but she did not feel rested, exhaustion slipping in and out of her consciousness and making her go cross-eyed with the effort of focusing. Her head felt too leaden to lift itself up and when she tried to focus on what to do next, her thoughts swam slowly away.

When she creaked her bedroom door open again she startled. A small someone was sitting on her rose sheets, dangling his legs off the bed.

"James," Aisha greeted him, after clutching at her heart.

"Hello, Aisha!" James called out. "I'm supposed to call you down for lunch."

"Thank you, buddy," Aisha said tiredly. "I'm very much called down."

James kicked his heels onto the bed frame some more. "Were you nice to June?" he demanded. "Because she looked like she'd been crying last night. I don't like seeing June cry."

Aisha wondered how much James remembered his mother. "No," she assured him. "Or, well, yes, but she was crying because she was happy." Not really, but her head weighed too much to explain this properly. "We were happy because it was the first time we'd talked to each other in a long time."

"Oh," James said, accepting this explanation without question. "Then that's okay. June cries at everything. She says everyone should always eps-express their emotions."

"I know that very well, buddy," Aisha said. "Hey." She thought of Esah, hollow and blank for years. "You know June cares about you very much, right?"

James sniffed. "Of course I know that," he said with an air like he feared Aisha knew very little. "She loves me, she always tells me. It's why we're building the big big bunker, because she loves me so much she wants me to be safe."

"Oh," Aisha said. James with his bright eyes and his short legs kick-kick-kicking, believing in nothing else but the strength of June's protection.

"My mama loves me too, June says," James offered, obviously finding Aisha a suitable candidate for a friend now he was quite sure she hadn't hurt June. "But she had to leave because she got sick."

"Your mama does love you," Aisha said, feeling something suddenly tear and tear and *tear* inside of her, shocking her into sinking onto the bed. "Very much."

"Yes I know, I just said that," James said exasperatedly. "Weren't you listening?"

James had moles down his neck and pushed his hair frequently back. Which parts of him were his mother? His mother who had had to leave, who had left James with someone who would love him and care for him. Was this before or after she knew there was no point? That there was no future for her son? Aisha could not really think past this new grief she felt for this woman. She hurt, suddenly and surprisingly. Nonsensically, she felt ripped apart.

"Anyway," James said, impatient, "I'm hungry so I'm going downstairs, you better come down soon or the food will be all finished because I'm so hungry."

Aisha managed an "Okay," and watched James kick the bed frame a few more times before heaving himself off it with a gusty sigh and saying, "Bye!"

"Bye, James," Aisha said. Something tore and tore inside her, ripping all the new skin apart, and she found she could not follow.

Moving In

(eight years ago)

Esah said, "I can't stay here." It was the end of the discussion. A matter of weeks later they stepped out of the taxi and stared at the little house, three months before Aisha's tenth birthday. It was two storeys and rather square, like a child's drawing of the house. The walls were a soft blue and the front door was lime green. There was a little patch of dry, browning grass in front. Wire netting knotted itself rather meanderingly about the house, a placeholder for a fence.

When Esah took that first step it was easier to take the second. Aisha stuck her thumb into her mouth and followed, but it was June who led, pushing open the wire netting and taking the first step into the house.

Aisha toed off her shoes and followed.

June said, "Look how nice this is! Look at these solid floorboards and look at that cosy kitchen," and she kept up that steady stream of talk, taking pictures and providing commentary. She pointed out the already-provided sofa and the "charming and vintage and old" television with the spiky, spindly antennae. She strode up the stairs and called downstairs to Aisha concerning dibs on the bed by the window, the one with the "really cool" view.

Aisha kept her thumb firmly in her mouth until Esah told her exhaustedly, "Take it out." Her mother sat on one of the rickety-looking kitchen chairs, her elbow propped upon its back and her forehead propped upon her fist.

Aisha took it out. Esah did not acknowledge this; she did not even look up.

June continued, "And the bathroom is so– so– *clean*, and the bidet is fully working and . . ."

The kitchen was so silent, even with June's voice calling from different corners of the house. It looked so different from the kitchen in Kuching, with its bright clean tiles and sprigs of flowers everywhere, its large windows and Pak's old pipe. That house had always smelled like something was baking in the oven.

Aisha said, "I miss Pak!" and felt horribly like crying. The past few weeks felt like they were coming to an awful, heavy head, and she wanted to cry; she wanted to sob; she wanted to scream and have it be heard. She wanted to go back home. They weren't going back home. This thought – this final straw – made the tears come; they welled up, slow and agonising, and started to fall quicker and quicker. Aisha looked at her mother through a blurry veil, and wanted to be held.

Esah didn't look up, even though she must have heard Aisha's breathing, hitching and hiccupy. Aisha tried to stop – *We've got to make it easier for her*, June said, in her head – but the lump in her throat wasn't going away. She clenched her fists and tried to get control back, crying as quietly as she could.

When it finally worked, when Aisha was furiously wiping away the wetness on her cheeks and swallowing around the rest of her tears, Esah got up. She put her hands briefly on Aisha's shoulders, more instruction than comfort, and only said, in a voice with no emotion and which brooked no argument, "We have to start cleaning up." She still was not looking at Aisha.

When Aisha got up, her mother steered her towards the stairs, and Aisha followed without question.

She knew by now that this tone of voice meant she must not upset her mother further, otherwise she would only go more blank, hollowed-out. She had stood like that over Arif's grave and she had not wept, even as distant far-spread relatives had sobbed around her. She had gotten home and not wept, even as June cried throughout every dinner and Aisha had looked around at the once-familiar kitchen with its once bright tiles and its wilted sprigs of flowers, feeling lost and adrift. She had decided to go across the country and not wept, even as June had said, increasingly more distressed, *No, no, no*, and Aisha had thought, increasingly more distressed, *No, no, no*. Esah had flown them over here and she had moved them into this strange house with the bright green door that seemed to mock the Arif-shaped hole in their lives and she was steering Aisha firmly up the stairs, and she was still not weeping.

The Truth, Encore

(the present)

The pure and simple truth was that Aisha was angry at everything. She was angry at the sun sputtering out and the great large hole in the yard. She was angry because she was beginning to care where Fleabag was when he wasn't around and she was angry at James's short, sure legs. She was angry for Elizabeth and Robert's lovely garden and the photo albums she had been going to show her grandchildren. She was angry for that house in Ipoh where Walter had toddled on small soles and the beach in Penang that felt like a living memorial. She was angry at Walter because how could you know you were going to lose someone you loved so deeply and keep on living? How could that someone bear to leave you, even for death? How did you stop being angry at them even when you knew they had no choice?

She was angry at her sister and she was angry at her mother. She was angry because she had never learned how to mourn.

She had not been taught to grieve her father. And if she had not even learned to grieve him, or anybody who she loved and who died, how could she begin to grieve the world ending?

Aisha pressed her forehead to her solid wooden head-board and thought about how the end of the world was predicted to play out. She thought about fire and smoke and waves and the earth cracking and moving, distressed. She thought about unlight. She was angry, so, so angry.

Esah had finally wept, seeing June. June cried every day, probably.

Aisha was *furious* that she wasn't crying.

It wasn't white-hot anger now either, the kind that rose

up sharp and jagged. This anger pressed slow and heavy and damply down on her.

"Oh," she said, and had to catch her breath, and catch it again. "Oh," she said, and felt so very hollowed-out with it. Arif used to read to her: her father had put his big solid bear arms around her in her bed and his voice had been low and steady. He had wasted away into skin and bones. He had wasted into the earth.

"Goodnight Moon," she said rather hysterically.

She wondered if she wanted to stamp her foot, or punch the headboard, and tried both experimentally, with no heat behind it. The wooden floor thudded and her knuckles hurt. Maybe this was not *anger*, or if it was, it was so heavy and yet carved something so wetly empty in her at the same time.

Fleabag meowed and meowed all the damn time and if the world cracked apart, who was going to feed him then? That stupid cat was curry-coloured and not even the good kind of curry, he was like curry which had gone off, and

Walter had gone and given permission for him to come home. Fleabag probably had sixty-seven bastard children, and none of them would survive. He had been in thirty-two fights and was going to go be a doctor and none of that would matter.

Aisha tried to breathe. She could barely manage it. She lifted her fingers again and curled them to her palms, squeezing hard, feeling the slight sting of it so she knew she was here, she was still here. There was a thickness in her throat and a wildness in her head. She hated this day. She hated how the day would end and there would only be a small number of them left. She hated her mother and her sister because loving them seemed very hard at the moment.

She lay down and *hated*, angrily and heavily and damply. There could have been hours in which she hated, she could not tell. She closed her eyes and felt jagged with hatred, her throat choked up with it, something violently clawing to get out.

What did escape, in the end, was an inadvertent and inarticulate sound. Aisha wasn't expecting it: the suddenness of the sound, the brokenness of the note. But once it had escaped others followed, feral and ugly, unable to be contained, impossible to control. Pressing her hands to her face to stifle the noise she realised the dampness all over was no longer just internal ache. Tears were making her face damp. They were streaming down her cheeks.

She was crying, she thought with some surprise.

No – that wasn't right. She was sobbing, suddenly. She was sobbing, wildly and brokenly, louder and louder. It was the kind of wailing that meant you had to kneel, curling in on yourself to ward away the pain. It was more howl than anything else.

The tears did not stop. Her head hurt with it but she could not stop, breathless and gasping.

Aisha cried. Time had come to a standstill. She didn't know how long it had been, but she was clutching at her blanket in fists, feeling absurdly like she was drowning.

She wanted to be held. She thought she might die if anyone saw her like this.

There was snot on the blanket, she realised eventually, breath shuddering. This distant observation helped her come to herself a bit more. Moving, limbs heavy, into a sitting position, she reached for a tissue and wiped at the blanket. She blew her nose, over and over again. Her head hurt.

When she could inhale through her nose, she lay down again.

In her sluggish head the waves came in, came out, came in again, calming her slightly.

The sun's rays died in golden bursts. Walter lay on the towel and she couldn't see his eyes, but knew they were soft brown, almost amber in the light. He built a fort with his sure fingers and scooped sand out of its moat, asked her for an ice cream, took her face in his warm gentle hands. In her head the waves came in, came out, came in again, never stopped. The sun was always on the verge of going down.

A Day of Sleep

(the present)

Aisha opened her eyes and felt empty. She didn't know how long she had slept. James came back up again and knocked on the door, probably with his feet from the way the thumping seemed to come from ground level, and Aisha called out, "Be down in a bit!"

She had no intention of being down in a bit. She was lying curled up on the bed, utterly exhausted, the anger that was left draining her dry. She felt like a husk of— something. She didn't even feel like a husk of herself.

June came to knock next. She knocked twice: Aisha

imagined her, her ear at the door, pushing back pink hair to listen closely for sounds of life.

"Sha?" she said. "You coming to eat?"

"Not hungry," said Aisha, trying to inject some energy into it so June wouldn't keep asking. "Keep it for later?"

There was a pause.

"Okay," June said hesitantly, like she was struggling to speak the language of Aisha again.

Aisha moved her head off the pillow, exhausted with the energy of keeping it on it.

She must have dozed off a little. When she woke up again it was late afternoon and Esah was knocking sharply at the wood of the door, each thud reverberating through Aisha's skull.

"*Sayang*," she said. "Are you okay?"

"Yeah, Mak," Aisha said, "just a bit tired." Her voice felt rusty and it felt like too much effort shaping words.

"Because you haven't eaten," Esah said. "I'll go get some food."

Aisha didn't answer, not because she was trying to be rude but because it was too much energy.

"You need water," Esah decided, and went away.

When her footsteps came back Aisha said, "Please leave it outside? I'm going to take a nap."

There was no answer. That was good. But before she could doze off properly again someone knocked.

"Aisha?" Elizabeth said.

Aisha schooled her voice to be as polite as possible. "Yes, Auntie?"

"I'm leaving a plate outside," Elizabeth said. "Just for whenever you need a snack."

"Thank you, Auntie," Aisha said, exhausted and surrounded by kindness. Exhausted because she was surrounded by kindness.

She took another nap. She didn't wake up to knocking this time, but there was someone outside. She could tell.

"Walter?" she said, a not-so-wild guess.

"Ah, what a surprise," Walter said.

"I'm really fine," Aisha said.

"No, you're not," Walter said. "That's fine, I don't want to talk about it either. But you should really eat or drink something."

"Not hungry," Aisha said tiredly, but she was tired of being not hungry also, and tired of everyone interrupting her tiredness. Her head felt very heavy but she lifted it and all her limbs too, concentrating on each one. She opened the door and Walter, holding a plate of food, re-adjusted his balance.

He offered the plate and the cup of water to her. There was another plate outside, full of cut fruit, and he brought that too.

"My mum," he said needlessly. "You look like a mess," he commented, after a moment of looking her over.

"Thanks for that," Aisha said, sinking onto the floor. When he sat down next to her, she pressed her face into his neck.

"Okay, no sleeping, let's eat," Walter said. She felt some movement and heard some clinking and he gently pushed her back, enough to hold a spoon between them. "Open wide now."

"Hey," she said. "I'm not a child." She let him push the spoonful into her mouth anyway.

"Yeah, yeah," Walter said, scooping up another spoonful of rice and *rendang*.

It felt so absurdly nice all of a sudden, being taken care of like this. Walter murmured things like "Here's another bite," and "There we go," and Aisha thought about feeling weak and pathetic and instead felt very grateful and taken care of. Everything about this was repetitive and felt like the steady dependability of the tide.

"We wouldn't have broken up if the world hadn't ended," Aisha said abruptly. "I just need some, I don't know, therapy." The word felt alien to her. She hadn't really thought about the idea except for some distant future notion. She tried to dismiss it, now, as something that would never happen, something that didn't bear thinking about. "I would have needed some either way."

Walter furrowed his brow and said nothing, so Aisha continued. "I wouldn't blame you if you left me now, though, for how I've been acting."

It was nice when he said, "Can you stop being silly?" and fed her another spoonful. "I've invested too much into this relationship now. Sunk cost and everything." He smiled at her, clearly just trying to get her to smile back. His crooked canines flashed. He loved her, and she knew this. It was so nice. It was just so nice.

"Did you know," he said casually after a bit, "that I'm angry too?" He sounded conversational, like he was talking about the weather.

Aisha took a moment to think about this. "No," she said plainly. "Sorry, I– I know it's selfish. I just haven't considered it."

"Of course I am," he said. "What's not to be angry about? Did you know I won't finish my bucket list?"

Walter, writing it out a month ago, head bent over the moleskin notebook and pencil firm in his hand, hadn't shown any inclination that he expected there to be a future where he wouldn't be completing each item.

Aisha didn't answer. She didn't want there to be a future in which Walter could not do every impossible thing on it.

"Well I'm not," Walter said, perfectly blunt about it. "I don't know who I was going to be. I wanted to try out every single thing, and I can't, and now I'll never know. It's infuriating." He was still talking in a deceptively calm voice, but his eyes were hard, staring holes into the doorframe beside them. "And then, you know, there's you, the only thing I'm sure about, and I won't get to have that either. I'm incensed."

He stopped talking then. He gently fed her another spoonful.

Aisha tried to reconcile this with Walter's warm eyes and endless patience, the way he wouldn't raise his voice even when she was snapping and he was curt, and found that she couldn't.

"You don't seem angry," she said, swallowing around

the spoonful, trying to say it carefully. If he was angry, it wasn't anything like her anger.

"I don't," he said. "It's still there." He shrugged, scraped the spoon against the plate, and said easily, "I just don't fight with you because of it."

Aisha supposed she deserved that. "Sorry," she said. "I don't mean to."

"I'm just incredibly mature," Walter said carelessly. "It's unfortunate you have to compete with how emotionally intelligent I am." Softer, he said, "Of course you didn't mean to. I hope you try very hard not to any more. Here's another bite." He fed it to her and brushed his knuckles affectionately along her cheek.

This brief touch was incredibly comforting. It lingered deliciously. Aisha longed to touch him, too, so she did, reaching for his beloved, familiar skin.

"I'm tired," Aisha said, after the food was done and she'd drunk her fill of the cup.

"Go to sleep, then," Walter said gently. He got up and made sure the fan was on, the pillow was plumped, that she was tucked in. He was right there. He'd always been.

She felt like she had when she was a child – a much spoiled, cherished child, doted on by Pak and indulged by her grandparents, protected by June and loved deeply in every moment by Mak. The feeling surprised her, and she wondered briefly if she was being patronised to, but it was so comforting that she didn't really care. Maybe this was just what people felt like when they were beloved. Like the people who loved them wanted to take care of them just as you would the tender wonder of a child.

It was like something had cracked and the feeling was the only thing that was shining through.

"I love you," Aisha said. For once she did not think about their lost future and the progression of the years they could have had. The only thing to focus on was Walter's soft eyes, melting her into easy sleep.

"I love you," Walter returned, lovely and easy as

breathing. Like it was a fact of the world. Like it might even live on even when no one was left, survive as a truth even when everything was going, going, gone. Aisha breathed in and out, and then she slipped into unconsciousness.

Goodnight, Stars

(the present)

When she woke this time it was night. It was night and she could see the dark night sky serene through the window, and Walter asleep in the armchair, like a faithful old guard. She draped a blanket over him and he didn't stir. She wedged a pillow between his cheek and his shoulder and he mumbled something incomprehensible, snoring starting up again. Aisha quietly opened the door.

The house was silent. She tiptoed downstairs and got a drink, the tap loud in the dark, water thudding against the sink. She drank thirstily from it. When she was done, she heard low voices in the back.

Aisha opened the back door.

Esah and June were lying down by the hole, talking lowly and looking up at the sky. The hole looked slightly larger than it had yesterday. They saw her and their words stilled, the murmuring coming to an end.

Aisha was tired, or she was finally awake. She crossed the garden and they moved to let her between them. She lay down on her back, grass prickly at first but shifting against her shirt, and looked up into the sky as well.

Stars winked back endlessly.

Like this, all Aisha could hear was the low, secretive chirping of crickets.

"I've been worried about you, *deng*," Esah said finally. Aisha couldn't see her, but she could hear the clear regret in her voice.

"I'm fine," Aisha said automatically.

"*Mun sik sikpa*. I know a lot of it is my fault."

"You know, you kinda messed us up, Mak," June said, kind of wetly. She shifted so that her pink head was pressed against Aisha's. She smelled strongly of vanilla tonight, like her room had always smelled. June didn't change much. She hadn't changed much.

"She was doing her best," Aisha said, and she believed it. She really believed it. She always would.

"My best could have been better," Esah said matter-of-factly. "I had two children."

"You were grieving," Aisha said. If it had been anything like today. If Esah's life had been just endless days like today, after Arif, and she'd just continued on, *how* had she just continued on . . . ?

Esah shook her head. "I wasn't grieving. I was, but it was more than that. *Sikda apa.*" She put her hand to her breast. *Nothing.* "*Dalam tok.* I couldn't feel anything most of the time. But I was so tired all the time. I wanted to sleep all the time. It was like I had stagnated."

It was what Aisha had known. It didn't hurt any less hearing that her mother had not felt much for half of Aisha's life, been numb throughout birthdays and

231

important milestones, her secondary school graduation and her badminton tournaments.

"I hadn't, though," Esah said, cutting through her thoughts. "I had you. You two. You two were growing up." She breathed in deeply and let out a long, long breath. "You were growing up. I couldn't handle it. Not without him. Every day was a day he'd never see."

Did you see? Aisha wanted to ask. *But you were there. Did* you *see?*

As if she'd heard her, her mother said, "It wasn't like that all the time. You were wonderful. Both of you. It got better, eventually. It did," she repeated, as if she could tell this reassurance was badly needed, wasn't enough, badly needed anyway. "Much too late. Now that we don't have any . . ."

When Aisha turned her head slightly to look, Esah was looking fixedly at the sky.

"I've been so proud of you," Aisha's mother said. "You should know that. Both of you. *Anak mak.* I haven't done the best job of showing it."

The stars twinkled benignly back down at her.

"But we do have time," June said suddenly, sitting up. Her hair glowed in the moonlight. "At least tonight we have time." She looked at Aisha. "We should catch up. We should talk. We have time."

"What do you want to talk about, Aisha?" Esah asked, and her voice sounded slightly scratchy: Aisha wondered how long June had been with her out here under the stars. She almost said it didn't matter.

It did, though.

"I don't—"

"You do know, though," June said, and Aisha hadn't missed this – this stupid bossy big-sisterly thing she could do and would do. Or maybe she had missed it, but June would never know. "And you deserve to know. Ask her."

Aisha closed her eyes.

"Tell me about Nek Dan and Nek Kah," she said. "Tell me about Pak, tell me everything, I want to know." She felt almost embarrassed, she sounded so greedy saying it like that: *I want to know*. But Aisha was allowed to want to remember, and she was allowed to know. She was allowed to ask for this.

"Okay," her mother said, "okay." Esah closed her eyes briefly and looked up at the night again. Her lips briefly shaped something silent, something neither Aisha nor June could catch. Perhaps a prayer. Perhaps something beloved to someone gone. She opened her eyes and started talking.

She told them stories: some Aisha had heard over and over again from June, like the way Nek Kah gave food freely away to *kampung* folk who used to come to the house and coo over Aisha, the way her plants flowered year-round and the way she'd handed down that recipe book to Esah. The way Nek Dan would pore over the newspaper and rant to the family over opinion articles at breakfast, and how he'd drive Esah, and then June when she was old enough, to get *kuih* in the *kampung*. She talked about Arif's bedtime stories and how he got June those first pink highlights even as Esah scolded, and then he'd coaxed Esah into laughter instead.

She told the stories that June and Aisha only vaguely remembered: Arif's Star Wars memorabilia he'd had to sell off when things were tight before Aisha was born, and how he mourned that Death Star model for weeks. And Nek Dan's old car, the Bluebird, how he'd take pictures of it and develop them, that prized blue thing. Nek Kah's ending up with a back problem from carrying Aisha around so much, how she did not let it stop her one bit until she'd had to be hospitalised. In the hospital bed her arms reached for Aisha and she'd said *Worth it*.

And then there were the stories June and Aisha had not known at all: Nek Kah's first and second miscarriage, how some days of the year she would go out and tend to two trees, the rambutan and the mango, the ones she had planted for her lost children. How once Nek Dan had scared a bear off just screaming at it in fear, and he'd gone home and proposed to Nek Kah just because he'd felt he could do anything, right then. Aisha had not known that before she was born money was tight and Uncle Amin had said to her father, *Don't have another, not right now,* or that when he'd first met her he'd said, *Never mind, you were right, what a miracle.* June had not known that Arif had stayed up three nights straight when she'd had jaundice, even as everyone else collapsed into exhausted sleep around him. They had not known exactly how Esah and Arif had met, but Esah told them what he was wearing that day and the way her stomach seized up with nerves, the way he'd grinned, young and lovely, and what they'd eaten at the lunch they'd had with their friends later in the day. They hadn't known the way the house in Kuching looked on their wedding day, filled and blooming with white flowers; they hadn't known the pure happiness of the look on Arif's face. They hadn't known that before he died he'd called out for his girls and then stopped Esah when she'd gone to get them, because he hadn't wanted their last memories of him to be of his death.

She remembered it all clearly, her voice meandering its way across the space to them. She said, "I thought I had so much time," again and again. "To write them down. To hand them to you properly. But now there's nothing left."

Esah looked to her children. Her gaze felt heavy on Aisha's face. "I still want to go back," she said. "*Balit rumah.*" The only place that would be home to her. Kuching.

Her voice shook and grew hoarse but it carried on. This should have hollowed her out even more, all these stories that had chafed her so emptily clean all these years, but as she spoke she became *more*, her short quick fingers gesturing to fill the spaces in her words and making nets of story all around them, her language shifting and sliding into Sarawakian, English, Malay. She had so many memories, Aisha realised. Not one of them forgotten. Aisha could have felt resentful that these had not been handed to her earlier but she could only wonder: where had she put them for so long?

She thought about her mother holding onto them

so desperately in her bones, the only place left after she had been hollowed out, and that heavy wet empty feeling pressed all around again.

This could not be *anger*.

Aisha knew if she lifted her fingers to her eyes they would come away wet. It was a strange, quiet kind of crying; she did not even know she was doing it. It wasn't the noisy, painful affair of last night. This was the sort of crying that didn't hurt.

These stories would not live on, Aisha thought. But did it matter? Here, in the night sky, these words wound themselves up into the stars, and the stars would keep them, and the stars would tell the waves, and the waves would come in, come out, come in again, even after they were gone. And even if that meant nothing, and these stories did not live, they lived *now*.

Wasn't that enough? It would have to be. They would make it enough that these stories lived now.

A Dream, Part Three
(a hypothetical present)

Aisha studied her new room.

Her sheets were blue. They were a light, cool blue, and they went with her poster of *Ms Purple*, up on the wall above the desk. There was also a corkboard up on that wall, and Aisha had Polaroids on it. Pictures with her mum, pictures with Walter, pictures with friends. To the bottom right there was an old one of her and June, sticky chocolatey ice-cream grins on their faces.

Aisha had also strung up fairy lights. Later on in the dark when she was feeling homesick, they'd bathe the room golden. But for now the large window let afternoon light stream through, and everything glowed with it. When she looked outside there were people sitting on the grass. Fragments of conversations floated up to the room: "But with all that," someone was saying, "how do you have the time for any . . ." Aisha looked at their bright upturned faces, ready for the next three years of their lives.

Aisha studied her room. She looked at the tiny closet and the creaking bed and the ancient-looking desk. There was a mysterious unseemly greyish spot on the wall she'd probably cover with another poster. She looked at her room and thought with satisfaction *this is mine.*

Aisha went to classes. She arrived twenty minutes early for her first class and made awkward eye contact with the girl who'd arrived twenty-two minutes early. She took classes and learned about human anatomy, pharmacology, medical ethics, brow furrowed into the night trying to understand. She made conversation out on the grass and she joined too many societies. On her father's birthday she spent the day in bed, then got up to cook *ayam masak lemak*, Arif's favourite. She remembered how he'd inevitably spill a bit on the tablecloth each time, wiping surreptitiously at it so Esah wouldn't see. She called Walter as much as she could and talked to him late into the night, shaping her day out in the kilometres between them.

Aisha went to classes. She made friends with the girl who always arrived early. They went out and explored the city, breathless and young with it. She took her classes and talked to patients calmly, kindly, frankly, trying never to forget this was someone worried, someone in pain. She attended society meetings and blithely missed more. During the holidays she visited Istanbul and Luxembourg, Belfast and Tokyo, Athens and Paris. She stood and stared out at grassy hilltops, ancient ruins, beautiful buildings; sat down at large farms, little cafés, museum benches, and tried to absorb the world. She put it off, but eventually she went to therapy and talked hesitantly, talked angrily, talked sobbingly. It didn't help for a long time, until one day she sat down and realised it had. She texted Walter throughout the day. She called Esah every week, like clockwork.

Aisha went to classes. She moved in with the girl who still always arrived early to every class. She left the room with the creaking bed and the mysterious stain and moved them to their little apartment, bringing her *Ms Purple* poster and her Polaroids with her. They watched movies late into the night, got irritated with each other over the dishes, made a roster and then some *matar paneer* because it reminded her roommate of home. She took her classes and cried in frustration about some of them, then took exams that turned out surprisingly well. She bought Nek Dan's favourite coffee-flavoured sweets and read Nek Kah's trashiest Malay novels. Sometimes she wondered if they would have been proud of the person she was becoming, and then decided, because she got to decide, that they would have been. At the end of her fourth year June turned up at her doorstep, longing and apologetic. Aisha hesitated for a long while, but she had been doing her work in therapy. She let her in.

Aisha went to classes, finished university, then she went out into the rest of the world. At work she talked to patients who were worried and in pain, and then she caught her breath in supply cupboards when she wasn't able to help them. She went home to the little apartment and watched more movies with the girl who'd arrived early in the classroom and become Aisha's best friend. She went out with other friends when she wasn't at the hospital, too, and they visited newly-opened restaurants and caught up on each other's lives, told stories about their week. In little ways she lived the people who were gone: the strength of her father, the quick tongue of her grandmother, the little squint she'd been told she inherited from her grandfather. The life she was living wasn't haunted, but she chose to remember her ghosts. She fought with and laughed with and grew with Walter, who came to see her as much as he could, in between trying to decide between a Masters in architecture or biology. She called Esah and June every week, like clockwork.

Aisha went to uni. She went out into the world. She went everywhere she could. In the mornings she blinked sleepy eyes open and listened to birds cry out, sweet and bright. She was living her life and oh, was she living it well.

Aisha

(always)

The next morning Aisha was up, very awake and very early. She washed her face and brushed her teeth and made her way down to the kitchen, tiptoeing past James's door. The adults were there already: Elizabeth in practical-looking trousers and Robert in an old T-shirt and shorts. Esah was scooping oats into bowls and June was sitting at the table. The blender whirred; Elizabeth was making everyone apple juice to start the day off right.

Walter yawned and slid into a chair, crooked canines exposed, cat-like. His warm fingers felt for hers and slid into them. Walter, here for whatever future she would have, doer of everything and anything that could be done. With him around this could wander into the realm of possible.

They trooped out of the house after breakfast and each went directly to their stations: Robert had the plans drawn up already, and he had assigned everyone a job. Elizabeth went with June to the metal sheets and Robert climbed into the excavator, looking right at home. Esah looked down at the plans and frowned, focused and very present.

Aisha looked at the size of it, the scope of what they were planning, and wanted to say something like, *Don't be so hopeful*. She wanted to say something like, *This might not work*.

But James's feet thudded, quick and noisy, down the stairs. There was a moment before he called out plaintively that he didn't want oats, he wanted eggs, and where *was* everybody anyway?

Elizabeth's photo albums were still at the bottom of her suitcase. June had the rest of her long, pink life left and Esah had to start living hers again. There was Walter, worth everything, and there was Aisha.

She picked a shovel up. It was oddly heavy, the wood slightly rough, the metal tip sharp.

Aisha struck it into the earth.

This was worth fighting for. *The power of humanity to come together and face what is to come is undefeated . . .*

Well, this was being brave.

Fleabag meandered into the backyard and they all yelled at him to go away. Hurt, he slunk back into the house, his old-curry coloured tail sticking sniffily into the air.

THE END

Acknowledgements

First, a huge thank you to Bella Pearson for the chance she took on me. She founded the marvellous Guppy Books, she created this competition which gives unpublished writers the opportunity of a lifetime, and she was with me for each step of the process of creating this book. I can't express enough how grateful I am for her invaluable advice and insight – working with her and her incredible team has been a dream come true.

Thank you to the talented Salvador Lavado for the stunning cover. It was everything I imagined – thank you especially for the brilliant interplay of colour and for making Fleabag look exactly as disdainful as I imagined him to be.

Thank you to Nate Ng for making the places I described come to life and stoically enduring my frequent revisions of your beautiful illustrations. We've come a long way from you stoically enduring me talking your ear off in class.

Thank you very, very much to my parents for everything they have done for me – I would not be anything that I am today without all they sacrificed for me. To my little sister: thanks for everything, I *guess*. I'm glad you exist, I *guess*.

Thank you to Nek Og, Nek Jeng, and Uncle Jim for being everything that they were in life: wonderful, constantly patient with me, endlessly loving. You live on in me, always.

To my housemates, thank you for not moving out when all I did was impose my questionable music taste on you and whine about writing (this gratitude is directed to all pseudo-house-mates as well.) To my law support group, thank you for never answering my messages and eating all my food, you've been very helpful. To my beloved friends from school that remain my friends: thank you for the fact that we check up on each other every half a year at most, but still I know you'll always be here for me. To the bro table, thanks for being up for every Discord call I suggest. To friends in various online communities, thank you for the encouragement that has motivated me to write for years. To the ladybug sibling society, thank you, thank you, thank you, I love you.

I would not have been able to learn to write if it hadn't been for the inspiration of people who write better than me. I am constantly inspired by well-known authors like Tolkien and Alcott, but also by authors who choose to have their works only on websites like ao3. Thank you for your world-exploring, it's where I learned to world-build.

To Snitch, Sykes, Larry, Quaffle, Deci, Dachi, thanks for being the cats I met along the way. Really sorry you had to go around the kampung with such unfortunate names.

This story is mostly about cats and people, but it's also about houses. There is much I could say about solid walls, history, and comfort, but I will simply say: thank you to anyone – family member or friend – who's ever let me in their homes.

To Zach, thank you for every instance of hope and healing this story holds. Thank you for everything else you've done and continue to do for me. I expect to be written about in your dissertation.

Nadia is a law student in London, a full-time houseplant owner and a part-time investigative journalist into what London's pigeons are planning when they flock together like that. She is mostly unsuccessful at (but still hopeful about) two out of three of these occupations.

She is from Sarawak in Malaysia, where the air is always sweeter, the food is always tastier, and the pigeons are considerably less bold. *The Cats We Meet Along the Way* is Nadia's first book.